A
DEEPER
DANGER

A DEEPER DANGER

A NOVEL

JEAN SPRINGER

Wolgemuth & Hyatt, Publishers, Inc.
Brentwood, Tennessee

The mission of Wolgemuth & Hyatt, Publishers, Inc. is to publish and distribute books that lead individuals toward:

- A personal faith in the one true God: Father, Son, and Holy Spirit;

- A lifestyle of practical discipleship; and

- A worldview that is consistent with the historic, Christian faith.

Moreover, the Company endeavors to accomplish this mission at a reasonable profit and in a manner which glorifies God and serves His Kingdom.

Unless otherwise noted, all scripture quotations are from the New King James Version of the Bible, © 1979, 1980, 1982, 1984 by Thomas Nelson, Inc., Nashville, Tennessee and are used by permission.

Wolgemuth & Hyatt, Publishers, Inc.
1749 Mallory Lane, Suite 110
Brentwood, Tennessee 37027

Library of Congress Cataloging-in-Publication Data

Springer, Jean
    A deeper danger : a novel / Jean Springer. — 1st ed.
       p. cm.
    ISBN 1-56121-024-2
    I. Title
  PS3569.P683D4 1990
  813'.54 — dc20
                                      90-34875
                                         CIP

Dedicated to my husband,
for a patience that is stronger
than my writing obsession

P R E F A C E

T hailand is a beautiful country with people as prone to
good and evil as those of any other nation, and there is no
intent in this story to malign anyone. The setting is moulded
from personal memories of south Thailand, but all of the charac-
ters and events are purely fictional. It is simply a tale of romance and adventure, one which I hope you will enjoy.

CHAPTER 1

*For death has come up through
our windows . . .*

The Prophet Jeremiah

T he dark silhouette of a man's head moved furtively into
the open, unscreened window; sinister eyes held a glint of
satisfaction as they watched the figure of a man asleep on the
bed, unprotected by a mosquito net. Cautiously, a hand moved
through the window, tipped open a cloth sack, and gingerly
shook out a dark form which settled at the foot of the bed.

The pale sliver of the tropical moon produced just enough
light to follow the ebony blotch as it spilled out over the white
sheet, uncoiling its body into a fluid, black streak.

Jonas Adams stirred in his sleep, irritated by the weight of
something draped over his ankles. A sluggish thought filtered
through his tired mind: a night breeze had moved the sheet. In
the next instant, his eyes flew open. There was something moving around his ankles all right. And it was twisting and turning
up over his feet. Lying rigid in the darkness, and realizing the
danger he was in, he suppressed the disgust seeping through his
body.

Snake! his mind roared.

ᴥ   ᴥ   ᴥ

Miles away, someone else was touched by the danger Jonas
faced.

"No!" The sharp word filled the hot Bangkok night around
her. Elizabeth Thurston wasn't sure why she had cried out, but
she slapped a hand over her mouth and sat straight up in bed,
her heart pounding.

"An earthquake! Here?" she whispered, moving to sit on
the edge of the bed.

She sometimes had strange dreams, but not one of them
had ever seemed so real — as though she had been physically
shaken or called by name. Her concern for Martin and Jonas
had probably triggered a nightmare. Or was it a warning?

Running slender fingers through her short brown hair, Elizabeth wished she were already acclimated to Thailand. Even in
the rainy season, the night air hung heavy, and none of the
apartments were air conditioned; that was reserved for the of-
fices and station facilities.

Elizabeth slipped on a summer robe, slid the screen door
open, and stepped out onto the balcony. A hint of more rain
masked the gasoline fumes from the traffic-infested streets, and
the pungent smell of curry mixed with the fragrance of some
tropical flower growing nearby.

Leaning against the railing, she took a deep breath and reviewed the past month in east Asia.

She and her brother Martin had returned to Bangkok expecting to plunge right into their vocations: he as a pilot for Adams
Import, Ltd., she as a temporary staff member of the International Missions radio station. Instead, they had fallen into intrigue and danger, facing guns, killers, and kidnapping.

Shortly after arriving in Bangkok their passports were
stolen, and they narrowly escaped death when the old temple,
where they were being held, crumpled and sank into the flood

waters. All of this because the Red Tiger, a Chinese gangster, wanted to eliminate Jonas Adams and his Christian testimony.

And, as if all that weren't enough, her bitterness over a broken engagement had been challenged by the gentle, solid love of her brother's employer, Jonas Adams. Her fear of another rejection fought his determination to marry her.

"Please," she had insisted the day after the incident at the Bangkok airport when Jonas was almost killed by the Red Tiger, "let me have some time to get accustomed to . . . to Thailand again."

Jonas had caught her around the waist and pulled her close to his side. Dark eyes watched her guarded expression as he spoke quietly. "You'll have to trust me, Liz. You can't go through the rest of your life testing everyone's love, waiting for their failure to prove you were right all along."

Kissing her lightly on the lips, he teased, "You might as well get accustomed to my presence. We're going to spend some time getting to know one another."

But a telegram had put a stop to his plans. Its message, "Familiar old statue needs help," came from Maggie Hathway, Jonas's longtime friend who shared his love of Thai antiquities.

"That statue was stolen from the Thai royal museum the week before we arrived in Bangkok," Jonas had explained. "And there are too many thugs around who won't think twice about killing for it. If she has the statue, her life isn't worth a green coconut right now." He had already made his decision.

He and Martin would fly to Pattani, a town nestled near the south end of Thailand's long tail, and they would bring both the statue and Maggie Hathway back to Bangkok.

"We'll have better mobility if we fly down. Elizabeth, I don't want you along; it's too dangerous. Be back in two days — at the most."

Elizabeth stared out across the rooftops toward the city proper, a dense jungle of ramshackled huts and ultra-modern

buildings with hundreds of Buddhist temples and traditional
Thai structures mixed in. The two days had come and gone, but
the men had not returned to Bangkok, nor had there been any
news of them at all. "Tomorrow," she determined as she turned
back to her room, "I'm going to do something. I'm not sure
what — but something!"

Somehow, the decision to act still did not ease her premoni-
tion that the men were in danger. She fell asleep praying for
their safety.

❧   ❧   ❧

Far to the south in Maggie Hathway's stilted, rambling
house, Jonas stared in horror at the poisonous viper coiling
around his feet. A pale light flickered through the latticework at
the top edge of the walls. It was Martin silently moving toward
the bedroom they shared, carrying a lighted kerosene lamp.

Cautiously sliding his hands to the top of the sheet, Jonas
decided on the only course of action: to flip the snake off the
bed before Martin entered the room. Any sudden movement
could provoke the viper into striking or startle Martin into dropping the lamp and setting the house on fire. But it would have
to be one swift, sure movement; the snake wouldn't give him a
second chance.

What happened next was more natural reflex than carefully
laid out plan. The snake slithered up the side of his left leg, and
Jonas reacted. Gripping the sheet with both hands, he snapped
it hard, flipping the snake into the air. It landed with a soft thud
on the floor.

"Don't come in!" he called as Martin's shadow filled the
doorway. "There's a snake in here!"

The barefooted Martin calmly set the lamp on a table beside the door. "Where?" he asked, peering into the shadows

through wire-rimmed glasses and then softly answering his own question. "There. Along the wall. Under the window."

Jonas leaped out of bed and began rummaging around in his suitcase. "Keep an eye on it while I find my gun."

"Your gun isn't loaded," Martin reminded him quietly. Watching the snake glide into a corner, he stepped back and reached around the doorway for the walking stick he had seen in the hall. It was heavy and would make a good weapon.

"Martin, you can't kill it with that!" Jonas had his gun in his hand and was trying to get it loaded.

Neither of the men shifted their gaze from the corner for more than a split second, for that was all the time it would take for the snake to coil for a strike.

"Won't have too many tries," Martin muttered, moving to the center of the room with his weapon raised high.

"It's coiling to strike!" Jonas warned, staring into the semi-darkness at the moving target, its head smaller than a baby's hand.

There was a soft smacking sound as Martin struck his first blow. Stunned, the snake responded instinctively, but slowly, into a coil.

Jonas raised his gun, but the intermingling shadows of snake and man frustrated his attempt to fire it.

Martin struck again, slamming the heavy wooden stick down on the writhing snake several times, finally snapping the wood in two.

In the ensuing silence, the men waited for the final twitch that would signal the snake's death.

"Whew. Thanks," Jonas finally gasped on the end of a deep breath. He turned to put the gun away. "We'd better get rid of it. I'd hate for Maggie to come back to a snake-infested house tomorrow!"

Martin laughed. "Good thing Elizabeth isn't here. This isn't exactly one of her favorite creatures." He prodded the snake cautiously. "I hope Maggie isn't sentimentally attached to this particular walking stick. Have to buy her a new one."

Martin draped the dead snake over the broken weapon, carried it outside, and threw it under a bush. He returned to the bedroom with a number of questions on his mind.

"Jonas, was it an accident that it was in here? Does the rainy season drive snakes into the house?"

"That's possible. It's easy for them to get in—no screens and lots of openings," Jonas replied, pushing a shock of black hair from his forehead. "But I have a feeling this one was dumped. And I was dumb enough not to use the netting. Here, help me move the bed away from the window."

After they had rearranged the room for a safer night, Martin turned down the lamp and crawled into his bed, carefully tucking the mosquito net under the mattress. "Jonas, do you think the plane is safe? Awful lot of men snooping around at the airport."

"Some of that is normal curiosity," Jonas murmured.

"I'd feel a lot better if it were locked up in a hanger, not sitting out in a field," Martin mumbled, revealing more concern than his usual placid nature would intimate. "If you don't mind, I'll go back out there tomorrow and check it out."

"Good idea," Jonas responded. "And we can do a little snooping on our own. We'll make our presence known in town and see what kind of response we get."

"Be surprised if there wasn't something," Martin chuckled. "Somebody's going to be shocked to see we're still alive. Do you have the feeling we've been followed ever since we flew in?"

The bed creaked under Jonas's restless frustration. "Yes, and we can't do much until Maggie gets back."

Martin turned on his side, propped his head up, and looked over at his employer. "Got any ideas about Maggie?"

"No. The note said that she was making an emergency run to the hospital in Saiburi and wouldn't be back until tomorrow. I just hope it's true."

"She left in a big hurry," Martin said thoughtfully. "Food on the table. Plate still half full. A brief note."

Jonas didn't want to invent a crisis when there was none, but he did feel uneasy about Maggie's absence. "There isn't any way to tell if it was an emergency, or if she's really in trouble. And we can't telephone the hospital at night. We'll just have to wait until tomorrow."

He fell asleep fully aware that these two days in south Thailand had been ominous ones. Their presence had aroused a great deal of interest. Maggie Hathway was in the middle of intrigue over a priceless statue, and he couldn't believe the snake episode had been an accident. The days to follow would likely bring even more danger.

≥ ≥ ≥

At breakfast the next morning Elizabeth stared out a kitchen window at the small enclosure overflowing with greenery and flowers that separated the back property of the radio station from one of Bangkok's busy streets. Frustrated and apprehensive, she decided to call Jonas Adam's secretary and hurried into the front office. Reaching across an empty desk, her hand was arrested in mid-air by the sharp ring of the telephone cutting through the morning quietness.

She jerked the receiver to her ear. "Hello?" she said breathlessly, in her excitement forgetting to use a Thai greeting. But the voice on the other end of the line was in heavily accented English.

"You want investment in south," a man growled. "You must find."

"Wh . . . ? Who are you? What do you mean?" Elizabeth demanded, but the telephone went dead. She stared at the receiver in her hand. "The only investment I've got in the south is Jonas and Martin. I knew they were in trouble!"

"That settles it," she murmured, dialing the number of Adams Import, Ltd. "I'm going south."

Answering the telephone on the first ring, Joy Change was appalled at Elizabeth's decision. "But you can't go alone," she protested, her soft accent slurred with concern. Her employer's attraction to the young American had been obvious. After all, he had nearly been killed saving her life. "What would Jonas do to me if you came to harm!"

"Nothing," Elizabeth replied with a laugh. "Jonas knows how . . ." She had almost said "persistent," but she knew the word wasn't strong enough. "He knows how stubborn I am," she continued, taking full responsibility. "We've known each other about a month, and I think we've argued half of it!"

Unconvinced, Joy nevertheless agreed to call for a plane reservation. Cradling the receiver on her shoulder, she flipped through the pages of the telephone book.

"Elizabeth," she said, changing the subject abruptly. "I almost forgot. There's a package here for you. It was delivered this morning."

After she hung up the telephone, Elizabeth swung into action. Since she was not due on staff for two weeks yet, leaving for south Thailand would not really pose any problems for the station. She briefed the office manager on her plans, called a taxi, and within fifty minutes was pulling up in front of Jonas's business.

It was a striking building, and even in her haste she took an appreciative look at the glass front where merchandise was dramatically displayed in diamond-shaped areas. It was imposing and struck a sensitive cord in her artistic nature.

A worried Joy greeted her at the front door. "Come, please." The diminutive secretary motioned to her office at the back of the large display room. "I have tea waiting for you."

"And a package?"

"Yes." Joy shot her a distressed look.

Elizabeth slit the tape that protected the small box and opened the lid. It contained a flat piece of silver cocooned in cotton, about one inch wide and two inches long, with an idol etched on one side and a message in Thai script on the other.

"I'll bet this is part of that statue, Joy. Apparently someone wants me to take it south. But why?" Elizabeth asked as she inspected the silver closely.

Ignoring Joy's continued protests, she decided, strong-willed as usual, to continue her plan to fly to Pattani.

Joy reluctantly arranged for one of the employees to drive her to the airport, and that afternoon Elizabeth set out to deliver the silver piece and to find those "southern investments" alluded to by the anonymous telephone caller.

&ə &ə &ə

Jonas and Martin left the house at six o'clock the morning after the snake incident. "We'll get some coffee and a local sweet bread in a shop in town." Jonas grinned at his companion's lack of enthusiasm as he hailed a pedicab.

Martin yawned. Waiting until the cyclist had slowed to a stop, he stepped up into the passenger area and sat down, making sure there was room for his employer. He watched the muscles rippling in the thin legs of the pedicab owner as he pushed down on the bike pedals.

He shuddered as he visualized the drink Jonas meant to have for breakfast: a glass half filled with sweetened condensed milk and an equal amount of the strongest coffee in the world.

"Ugh," he groaned, "*kopi-susu* this early in the morning. Too sweet."

"Cheer up, Martin." Jonas grinned. "This is going to be a profitable morning."

"For what?"

"For planning against emergencies," came the emphatic reply.

Martin pulled off his glasses and rubbed his eyes, grunting at his friend's spirited appreciation of the "uncultivated beauty of south Thailand."

"Businessman," he mumbled good-naturedly. "Seen some local art that might be a hot export item?"

"Essentials first, Martin. We'll concentrate on getting Maggie out of here, then we'll tend to business."

"Where do you suppose she hid the statue?"

Shaking his head, Jonas laughed at the possibilities. "I haven't a clue, but knowing Maggie, she probably has it stashed right under the governor's nose, or in the United Moslem Front headquarters."

"That's one spirited lady."

"Determined is the word," Jonas complained. "She should have caught the first plane out of here. Instead she's stuck her neck out a mile, trying to save a statue!" The anger in his voice was only a hint of the frustration he felt. "We're going to get that woman out of here as soon as she gets back into town."

"If she gets back," Martin murmured.

"We'll check that problem out as soon as we've had coffee. I want to telephone the hospital and find out if she's there. If she isn't, she's in danger."

Martin settled back against the rattan contours of the passenger seat. "And if she's been kidnapped?"

Jonas silently searched for some answer but finally admitted, "There aren't too many things we can do but wait to be contacted, and . . ."

"And?"

"Well, first we'll try to find help, and then we'll provide some bait."

The help Jonas had in mind came from the young pastor of the Chinese church. Cordially welcoming them into his small apartment at the back of the church building, he listened intently to Jonas's plans. Yes, the local church loved and respected Maggie Hathway, and he knew of a man, just arrived from Bangkok, who would help in a rescue attempt if needed.

Jonas's bait turned out to be an unidentified object wrapped in newspaper, purchased at a local shop owned by one of the church members.

"Looks like a statue," Martin remarked after they left the shop.

"That's what I had in mind," Jonas mumbled, glancing at the Asian shoppers on the street.

Martin's slow smile spread across his face. "Show it off in town. The news gets back to the interested parties. They'll pay us a visit. Right?"

Jonas grinned. "Martin, my friend, for someone as placid as you are, I'm surprised you have such a scheming mind."

"Like detective stories. Anyway, *you're* not passive about life; you make things happen."

"Right again," Jonas agreed as they sauntered down the sidewalk toward the next shop. "I feel safer on the offensive." He shifted the package to his other hand and steered Martin down a side street. "Let's stop by the police station and call the mission hospital, then we'll put this in Maggie's front room and wait for a visitor."

ِ◆   ◆   ◆

Jonas and Martin took unobtrusive posts in the house where they could watch the front veranda. They waited three long hours in silent vigilance, occasionally taking turns patrolling the house, looking for possible intruders.

Then, without warning, gunshots sounded from the backyard, quickly followed by shouting voices.

Both men ran to the back door. Noisy, frightened neighbors were running through the palm trees, pulling children to safety and milling about the backyard. Some were sympathetic, some nervous, and some simply curious, and they were all chattering at the same time. It took Jonas several minutes of stern persuasion to calm them down enough to hear their individual responses.

"Well, we don't know what it was," one man admitted in Thai. "There was shooting, that's all."

"It was the police!"

"No, outlaws!"

"It was over by the mosque!"

No one knew anything definite. Suddenly Martin turned and ran toward the house, vaulting the steps in two jumps and disappearing inside.

Jonas stared after him for a moment. Then in a flash of realization he bolted after Martin, berating himself for falling for such a simple trick.

The wrapped package was gone. The confusion in the backyard had been staged.

C H A P T E R   2

*I have been a stranger
in a foreign land.*

The Book of Exodus

E
xcuse, please," a soft voice requested. Elizabeth turned toward her seatmate, a young Chinese woman dressed in a navy blue skirt and white blouse.

"Yes?" Elizabeth returned the woman's smile and waited.

"Sorry," the young woman ventured shyly in precise English. "I do not wish to trouble you, but . . ."

Elizabeth responded warmly to her hesitation. "What can I do for you?"

"My name is Su-Ling." Dainty hands clutched a black purse more tightly than necessary, and she nodded solemnly upon hearing Elizabeth's name. "My — ah — husband works in the city of Yala, but I have never been south. Could you help me?"

"I'm sorry. I've never been there, either," Elizabeth replied. Then, noticing the young woman nervously picking at the corner of her purse, continued reassuringly, "But, I'll be glad to help you all I can. There will probably be an agent at the airport who can tell you what to do."

"You are meeting someone," Su-Ling said, with what seemed like more purpose than curiosity in her voice.

"Yes." Elizabeth's response was uncharacteristically short. Her reluctance to disclose even the smallest bit of information to this stranger made her wonder if her recent Bangkok adventure had made her unduly suspicious. It wasn't considered impolite in Asia to ask such questions; in fact, asking personal questions indicated genuine interest. But she was still uneasy.

"I hope our flight isn't any longer than two hours," she said, using her artist's notebook as a fan. "I don't think the air conditioning is working."

She wore a cool, pastel cotton skirt and a wide silver belt, but her pale blue blouse was now sticking to the seat from the perspiration trickling down the back of her neck, and she felt the first signs of a headache tightening behind her eyes.

Su-Ling's smile contrasted sharply with the solemn look in her black, almond-shaped eyes. "It is warm," she agreed before resuming the questions. "You will work in Pattani?"

"No."

"Do you have relatives there?"

"My brother."

The small hands were stilled. "Ah. He is a teacher?"

"No." Once again Elizabeth changed the subject. Looking out the window she watched the Asian scene below.

"Thailand is a beautiful country, Su-Ling. You must be proud of it. The blue waters of the gulf, the fishing boats, the rice paddies, the mountains." She opened her pad and with a charcoal pencil began to sketch what she had seen. Smiling innocently at the perplexed look on Su-Ling's face, she chattered on about the Thai countryside.

A few minutes later she heard a child's voice and, glancing up, was delighted to see two little hands appear at the top of the forward seat, followed by a shock of black hair and a pair of black, mischievous eyes. She sketched the little boy's face, her pencil speeding over the page, then tore it out and handed it to him. Her reward was a big grin, and she turned to Su-Ling.

"I've always been intrigued by the different peoples in Thailand," she noted, nodding toward the other passengers. "There are Thai, Malay, Chinese, Sikhs, and Indians on board. I'm the only Caucasian."

"Yes," Su-Ling replied. "You are the only *farang* here. Does that trouble you?"

"No, there are so many friendly people." Elizabeth refused to admit, even to herself, that being the only foreigner on board did make her feel a little lonely, especially since she knew she had been lured into delivering the silver piece to Jonas. And, if that was true, it would only make sense to assume that she was being followed. Was it her seatmate who was so full of questions, or the two Chinese men across the aisle who had arrived at the airport in the taxi just behind hers? Elizabeth was sure they had been watching her the entire trip.

Su-Ling interrupted her thoughts to inquire about her purpose for living in Thailand, and Elizabeth again answered as briefly as possible and changed the subject. After a few more unsuccessful attempts to get information, Su-Ling gave up and, retreating into a polite silence, watched Elizabeth work. In a few minutes she appeared to be asleep.

What will I do, Elizabeth wondered, *if Maggie Hathway isn't at the airport to meet me? What if Jonas and Martin . . . ?* Shaking her head, she sat back and took a deep, calming breath.

Here is the perfect opportunity to learn how to trust God. It was all too human to insulate oneself from disappointment by expecting the worst; she would instead believe that good would come out of this trip to help Maggie Hathway.

Elizabeth wondered what the missionary was like. The name conjured up in her mind a middle-aged, slightly pudgy, weary looking woman. She was sketching a second possibility of Maggie Hathway's appearance when the warning light came on and the stewardess announced their approach to Pattani. They would be on the ground in less than ten minutes.

When the plane had taxied to a halt at the far end of the runway, Su-Ling refused Elizabeth's offer of help with a *mai pen rai,* wished her a safe visit, and with only her purse and a large straw tote bag, started down the aisle. For a moment Elizabeth stared after her in surprise, wondering why someone moving to a new city would have no more luggage than that. Then she remembered that Asians lived quite successfully with far fewer accessories than westerners.

Getting bumped by an impatient passenger brought her back to her own needs. She had to get off the plane and find Maggie Hathway! Drawing her shoulder bag tightly to her side and anchoring her purse strap around one arm, she pulled a small suitcase from the luggage compartment.

The moment her feet touched the ground it began to rain — the hard, pelting kind that had all the passengers ducking their heads and running across a wide open field toward the cement block building that was the local air terminal. She hadn't thought to bring an umbrella, and so she ran unprotected, holding her possessions as tightly as possible, concentrating on staying away from the two Chinese men.

She was surrounded by passengers, all of them ignoring everything else in their dash across the field. The umbrellas of protected passengers poured rain down in extra torrents on the less fortunate. A Chinese woman who dropped a package in a puddle yelled angrily at the man who impassively stepped on it. Startled at this complete disregard for others, Elizabeth was temporarily distracted from her own situation.

A moment later she felt a tug at her suitcase. Two thoughts flashed into her mind instantaneously: the warning in current travel books about the increase of crime in Asia, and the knowledge that local police could not always be counted on to help much. But she didn't plan to give up her suitcase without a fight. She hung on to the case, not caring how many people it struck. All that mattered was keeping her grip.

But the Chinese hand was stronger. The man jerked hard, expecting Elizabeth to lose her hold. But she hung on, falling sharply against his body. She heard his surprised grunt with great satisfaction. "Stop it!" she cried, and then, "Help me, please!" All the right Thai words fled from her mind, yet she knew that a few passengers would understand enough English to know what was happening. But no one wanted to get involved; Elizabeth was on her own.

With one swift downward movement, the man jerked the case free and shoved her into the crowd. Elizabeth fell to her knees, sending several other passengers sprawling out onto the wet ground with her.

Shouts of rebuke in a mixture of languages ensued, first at the Chinese man for shoving and then at Elizabeth for creating such chaos. Someone jerked her upright and effectively swung her to the edge of the crowd, where she would no longer trouble anyone.

Elizabeth fought down an anger bordering on panic. She was alone. And as soon as the thieves discovered the silver piece was not in the case, they would return. Of that she was sure. Equally certain that she needed to find her friends as soon as possible, she turned and ran toward the terminal building.

The rain, which as usual in the tropics had ceased as quickly as it had begun, had not cooled anything. Elizabeth, who had stopped just inside the terminal door, could hardly breathe in the steaming heat coming from the wet clothing and warm bodies crowding the room. Searching through the wild, noisy scene for the two Chinese men, she found only a room full of travelers, each trying to outdo the other in getting information, luggage, or help.

Not really expecting to find her assailants, for a fleeting moment she did think of Su-Ling and wondered why she wasn't there attempting to get help from a flight agent. It was unfortunate, Elizabeth thought while berating herself for not being more cordial, that she wouldn't see the young woman again.

She stood against the wall, soaked to the skin, simultaneously looking for friends, searching for help, and wiping the mud from her hands and legs. There was no one who looked remotely like a Maggie Hathway. Nor did she see a tall, rugged-looking Jonas Adams or a young man named Martin Thurston who bore a remarkable resemblance to herself. Her heart sank as she realized she was the only Caucasian in the building. Elizabeth struggled through the crowd, trying to make her way up to the counter to ask for help, but no one would let her through. There were no designated areas, no identifiable lines of people, yet she was completely ignored; it was as though she was invisible.

Finally, determined to locate the town's Provincial Police headquarters, she pushed through the crowd and out the front door and found two policemen leaning against the building. Their English was minimal.

"Police," they repeated as they pointed to their badges, and then broke into such rapid Thai that she couldn't distinguish even one familiar word. Except the word *farang*. She wanted to protest loudly that she was well aware of the fact that she was a foreigner, but she simply smiled and tried once more to make them understand what had just happened. When that failed, she tried to find out where police headquarters was located.

Knowing that it was considered quite rude to use a hand, Elizabeth followed the Thai custom and pointed with her chin toward the buildings down the street. She repeated her request, "police headquarters."

Again the men imitated her words, this time touching their guns, symbols of their occupation.

Thoroughly frustrated, she dug down into her shoulder bag to get a Thai dictionary, hoping to find the words for thief or police headquarters.

But something was wrong. Jerking the bag around for a better look, Elizabeth discovered that her Bible and sketch pad were missing. Probably disappeared in the same hands that stole my suitcase, she thought angrily.

To add to her difficulties, there was mounting confusion in the street as a large crowd gathered to watch. Most of them were Malay men, distinguishable by their long sarongs and black Moslem hats; they stared at the foreign woman, their suspicious nature rubbing like salt into Elizabeth's wearying sense of defeat. It was perfectly permissible behavior in Asia to openly watch others, but Elizabeth wanted to scream, to stop the unwavering stares, to stamp her foot and demand her right not to be viewed like some monster from the jungle.

To her horror, she realized that what she was actually about to do was cry. The painful lump in her throat was a sign she didn't like, and she took a deep breath and blinked hard, stubbornly refusing to indulge in the dubious refuge of tears. Determined not to be thwarted, she nevertheless realized she wasn't going to get any help from the two policemen. Defeated, she turned back toward the building, hoping to find someone who spoke English.

Suddenly, the welcome sound of her own native language stopped her, and she went weak with relief.

"Elizabeth," a voice called out.

Swinging around, Elizabeth found herself staring at the commanding appearance of an attractive American, and in her present state of mind, she felt like a gaping, scrawny child who had been pulled from a mud puddle to stand before royalty. It was no exaggeration to say the woman could have been a model—perhaps was one!

Long brown hair piled softly on the top of her head, the woman was dressed in a crisp, full-skirted yellow dress and carried a Thai umbrella against the rain. It couldn't be Maggie

Hathway! Not the Maggie that Elizabeth had conjured up on her sketch pad!

"Oh, Elizabeth, I'm so sorry to be late!. Come," the young woman said with a smile that lit up dark brown eyes. "We'll get you home immediately. You look exhausted."

"Maggie?" Elizabeth asked in disbelief. "Maggie Hathway?"

C H A P T E R   3

___

*And they will burn your houses
with fire.*

The Prophet Ezekiel

E lizabeth's mouth dropped open in complete surprise as she stared at Maggie Hathway. Why wasn't Jonas Adams married to this woman? But she didn't have time to ponder the question; apparently Maggie Hathway habitually landed at a scene with whirlwind force and immediately set about getting things accomplished. Elizabeth barely had time to greet the smiling missionary before she was hustled to a covered jeep, handed a sarong to dry her wet hair and clothes, and plied with questions about her trip.

Her replies were brief and to the point. "The flight was nice. Yes, I did meet someone: a young Chinese woman named Su-Ling. Yes, I did have trouble. Someone stole my suitcase just after we deplaned."

That brought Maggie's forward movements up short. With her hand on the ignition key, she stared at Elizabeth.

"Say that again."

"Two Chinese men watched me continually on the flight from Bangkok. One of them jerked my suitcase out of my hand when we were running through the rain toward the airport terminal."

"Could you identify him?"

"No," Elizabeth replied as she folded up the sarong and laid it on the back seat of the jeep. "He was short and stocky, but had no distinguishing marks of any kind."

"Are you sure?"

"Yes, I'm sure," Elizabeth answered with a smile. "I'm a portrait artist. I would have noticed anything unusual about either of those men."

At that, Maggie shoved the jeep in gear and, with a couple of quick blasts of the horn, pulled out into traffic. "We'll just see what the police say about this."

But it was a futile stop. The local police didn't seem concerned over the stolen suitcase. After all, the foreign lady had not been hurt, had she? Elizabeth felt Maggie's irritation as the woman graciously thanked the captain on duty, and with palms together and chest held high in the traditional Thai greeting, bowed slightly and said good-bye.

"Come on, Elizabeth," Maggie sighed as they shared her umbrella outside the station. "Let's go home and see if Jonas is there."

"And my brother Martin."

"Your brother?" Maggie asked, motioning to the right. They skirted a mud puddle and a parked pedicab before coming to the jeep.

"He's just become Jonas's pilot. They flew down here soon after your telegram arrived, promising to be back by last evening." Elizabeth dropped her shoulder bag into the back of the jeep, climbed into the passenger's seat, and glanced with concern toward the other woman. "Haven't you seen Jonas yet?"

"No, I've been out of town since yesterday morning." Maggie started the jeep, waited for a gap in the evening traffic, and then inched her way into the busy street.

"But how did you know I was arriving?" Elizabeth asked.

"The telegram came to the hospital this morning." Maggie turned to stare at her passenger, suddenly realizing the implications of what she had just said. "You sent the telegram to Pattani."

"Yes."

"And I got it in Saiburi, thirty miles from here. That means someone was being quite helpful." Maggie frowned, her voice full of irony. "I wonder who it was."

Light from open-front restaurants and stores spilled out in elongated patterns across the cement road, and pinpricks from the pedicab lights timidly prodded the darkness. They passed a theater where a Thai movie was showing, and the Oriental music blaring from the loudspeakers halted their conversation until they were into the next block.

"I'm confused," Elizabeth began when the music faded. "You asked Jonas to come, but you weren't in town when he arrived. Why?"

"I'm often asked to make emergency runs to the mission hospital. And under the circumstances I didn't dare refuse to go."

"Under the circumstances?"

"I'm watched constantly. I was afraid of arousing suspicion if I waited for Jonas instead of following my usual routine, so I went to the hospital."

"That makes sense," Elizabeth agreed, silently wondering what she would have done had she been as anxious to get help. As the present guardian of a piece of royal antiquity, Maggie was in a highly dangerous position. A number of factions could be fighting over that statue: Communists, Moslem insurgents, and nefarious gangsters, to name a few.

Apparently unconcerned about her problems, Maggie shrugged her shoulders and smiled. "Tell me, are you visiting Thailand?"

"No, my parents are missionaries up-country; Martin and I were practically raised in Bangkok. I've come back to work temporarily for the Christian radio station there. We flew from the United States with Jonas and got here ahead of schedule, so he was planning to spend some time with — with Martin and me." For some reason, Elizabeth was reluctant to tell this attractive stranger that she and Jonas Adams had become — what? A romantic involvement sounded like something out of a novel.

Elizabeth had to admit that it sounded impetuous. In just a few weeks that tall, rugged-looking man with all of his experience and abilities, had decided most emphatically that he wanted to marry her. He was a widower in his early thirties; she was a fresh college graduate recovering from a broken engagement.

She shook her head at the idea and kept her eyes on the scenes of Pattani. The town looked much like the business areas of Bangkok, except that here a throng of pedestrians and pedicabs replaced the swarm of trucks and cars that choked the streets of the capital city. Maggie inched the jeep forward, patiently waiting for a slow-moving pedicab driver to acknowledge her presence and cycle to the side of the road. She glanced at Elizabeth.

"I'm pleased you're here, and as a friend of Jonas Adams, you're doubly welcome. He's one in a million."

The word *friend* caught Elizabeth's thoughts, but she let it pass. It was Jonas's responsibility to inform Maggie of their relationship, especially since Elizabeth wasn't sure she could accurately define it at the moment.

Maggie went on. "I'm just sorry to drag you in on something that could be life-threatening."

Elizabeth raised a hand in protest and laughed. "I think danger is going to be part of my lifestyle from now on. I've known Jonas Adams for less than two months, and if I could gather up

my past troubles in a basket, it wouldn't weigh one-tenth of
what I've gotten into since I met him!"

She grew serious then. "He was certain you'd found the silver statue and was afraid you were in trouble. Do you really
have it?"

Maggie nodded, shifting gears as she turned a corner and
started down a quiet street that led toward the outskirts of the
city.

"Yes, I have it, and I still can't believe how it happened. I
was driving back from the hospital and decided to stop at a little village market about halfway home. I thought it was a good
time to make some new contacts. You know what the day markets are like — merchandise spread all over the place, in wooden
stalls, on pieces of cloth on the ground, anything and everything, everywhere. Well, I was just wandering around when I
spotted the statue. I couldn't believe it. A woman sold it to me
with no more interest than if she were selling bananas."

"But why?" Elizabeth pondered. "It doesn't make sense."

Maggie nodded. "That's what I thought." Her eyes were on
the road ahead. There were fewer buildings now, and it was a
lonely stretch of road. "Someone must have stolen it, tried to
bring it south, and in the process, lost it."

"Who would want it here? What good would it do?"

"Well, I figure it's either the local Communists or a Moslem insurrectionist group called the United Moslem Front. And
they'd both sell it to buy ammunition."

"But why bring it all the way south? Why not sell it in
Bangkok?"

"I've been wondering that myself," Maggie replied, "and I
think someone has a generous buyer just over the border, in
Malaya. Which leads me to believe it's probably the UMF
that's involved."

"Did you hide it in your house?" Elizabeth asked, concerned for Maggie's safety.

"No. Someone followed me home from the market. They knew I had the statue; I didn't dare leave it in the house."

"What did you do then?"

"I decided to move it as soon as possible, but there was the problem of where. I couldn't hide it in the church building or in one of the local Christian homes for fear of endangering them. And it would have been found in my house."

"It's been searched?"

Maggie nodded. "Ransacked," she said dryly. "Twice."

"So, where is it?"

"The only place I thought they'd never suspect."

"Where?"

Maggie glanced at her passenger with a grin. "It's safe — I hope."

Just then they drove past a large field, and a loud noise distracted Elizabeth's attention.

"What is that?!" she demanded, forgetting their conversation. "I didn't know there were herds of cattle in the south!"

Maggie laughed and slowed to a stop. "It does sound like cattle, but it isn't." She watched Elizabeth's face in the light reflected from the dashboard.

"But what else could it be?"

"Frogs."

"You're kidding!" Elizabeth looked suspiciously at her companion, questioning her sense of humor.

"It's a frog peculiar to this area, and it does sound like a cow."

"Good grief," Elizabeth groaned. "How can you get any sleep with all that noise?"

"Fortunately, there aren't any around my house. This is the one place along this road that's swampy enough for such a gathering."

Car lights appeared in the rear view mirror, and not wanting to be a sitting target, Maggie threw the jeep into gear and

sped along the road. "Even if I were blindfolded," she added
with a laugh, "I'd know this place. Now, along here," she motioned toward the left, "are rice fields and a number of small
Moslem villages beyond. My house faces this road and sits
right at the edge of a larger village, with a school across the
street. There's always plenty of activity going on."

"I can imagine," Elizabeth said with a smile.

Maggie checked the rear view mirror again and was relieved to see that the lights behind them belonged to a bus half
full of chattering women. "Perhaps you've heard that it's dangerous for our workers to live in the villages now. Moslem missionaries from the Near East are concentrating their efforts in
this area, and they've stirred up a lot of fanaticism."

In a few minutes she pulled off the road, drove the jeep
under a bamboo shelter, and cut the lights. Taking a flashlight
from under the front seat, she got out and guided Elizabeth toward the back veranda of a large wooden house.

At the back steps she slipped off her sandals, took a dipper
of water from a large earthenware jar, and splashed the dust
from her feet. Elizabeth followed suit, and in a moment the
women mounted the steps and padded silently across the veranda.

"The men must be here," Maggie remarked, relieved to see
a light in the kitchen.

Even in the dark Elizabeth could tell that this was an interesting house — a large, sprawling place with rooms jutting out
here and there and pointed, curved tips on the roof that charac-
terized the Thai architecture she so appreciated.

She was eager to see the interior. Surely such a pretty
woman would have an equally beautiful home! But even more,
she was impatient to see Jonas. And Martin, of course.

She followed Maggie in through the back door and with
one quick glance took in the kitchen. To her right were a work
table, stove, refrigerator, and several free-standing wooden cup-

boards. Then she looked toward the table at the left where the two men were seated. Martin appeared his usual placid self and seemed to be all right. She waited in the shadows, heart racing, and watched Jonas rise as Maggie approached the table.

There was always a brownout in the early evening when the demand for electricity was high, and in the dim light neither man had recognized her. She expected adverse reactions to her presence, but her defense was ready.

"Maggie, am I glad to see you," Jonas exclaimed, his voice full of warmth, his smile as eager as his embrace. "Sit down and tell us what's happened. I was afraid you might have been kidnapped."

Such a loving scene. Too loving, Elizabeth suddenly thought with alarm. The couple looked as though they belonged together: both a few years older than she, both experienced, competent in their work, both more a part of Thailand than she ever was as a child. She stepped forward into the light.

Martin noticed her first, his chair squeaking a protest as he stood up in surprise. "Elizabeth! What are you doing here?"

Elizabeth turned her eyes toward Jonas, silently waiting for his response, wondering if they would have another argument, and sensing something else in the pit of her stomach that she didn't want to acknowledge. It would be better to concentrate on defending her arrival than to wonder why she suddenly felt lonely.

"Hello, Martin," she said quietly, her eyes still on the other man. "Jonas."

Maggie sank down in a chair at the end of the table, thankful to have these two men in the house, and yet watching with puzzled interest as she sensed the bond between the young woman and Jonas. Already aware of Jonas's strong will, she now perceived a toughness in Elizabeth she hadn't noticed before.

She glanced at Martin. His unruffled spirit was soothing and tranquil, and she liked him immediately. Evidently whatever was taking place between her friend and this young woman wasn't upsetting Elizabeth's brother in the least. He glanced her way and winked.

At last Jonas moved forward, stopping just in front of Elizabeth. "You came anyway," he said softly, not touching her but still affecting her deeply.

"Yes." Her eyes searched his, looking for a sign of acknowledgement, of love, of something more than the waiting she felt. Taking a deep breath, she went on, her voice firm against the look Jonas was giving her.

"I had a telephone call . . . this morning . . . a warning about you and Martin. And then a package was delivered — to me. It had a piece of silver in it. I *had* to come."

"Jonas," Maggie interjected reprovingly, her voice breaking through the tension that held the couple in a separate world. "Jonas, bring Elizabeth here. She's exhausted and has had quite a welcome already."

"What kind?" Martin asked, picking up on the edge in Maggie's voice. Maggie explained about the stolen suitcase while Martin poured coffee for the two women and got them something to eat.

Meanwhile, Jonas had taken a chair across the table from Elizabeth, and he listened intently, occasionally asking a quiet question, as Maggie explained the events of the past few days.

"Why didn't you take a plane for Bangkok?" he asked when the woman stopped for a moment to bite into her food.

Maggie shrugged her shoulders. "The local Christians are getting ready for their first provincial conference. I'd promised to help and just couldn't leave them stranded."

Jonas frowned. "You can't do everything, Maggie, and at the moment, your first priority is your safety."

Not intimidated by his authority, the missionary replied calmly, "I thought that if nothing happened, I'd just wait and fly up after the conference was underway."

"But somebody's determined to get that statue," Jonas protested. "You knew you'd have trouble, didn't you?" He shook his head and went on. "You're so full of responsibility for others. Can't you use a little of it on yourself?"

"No more than you, Jonas Adams." Maggie smiled gently and reached out to pat his hand, obviously pleased at his presence and unperturbed with his scolding.

"Where's the statue?" he asked, giving her hand a squeeze before he reached for more coffee.

Maggie looked at Elizabeth and laughed. "Oh, it's closed up tighter than a drum."

"Now what's that supposed to mean?" Jonas frowned at the knowing look shared between the two women. He wasn't quite ready to forgive Elizabeth's disobedience, for her presence with them only magnified his concern for their safety.

"Maggie, you do realize, don't you, that you're up against something more than just a prankster."

"Of course, I do, Jonas. I've been followed everywhere, someone watches the house constantly, it's been ransacked twice, and I've had a couple of threatening notes. I'm just so relieved to see you two men, and I'm delighted to have Elizabeth here."

"And what now?" he asked with a slight smile.

"Well, in an hour or so, I'll go get the statue. And tomorrow morning we can all fly back to Bangkok."

"I'll go with you," Martin volunteered before Jonas could issue a command. He rather liked this spunky woman, and if she was brave enough to hide a valuable treasure somewhere under the enemy's nose, he would enjoy being involved.

"I accept," Maggie said, giving him a beautiful smile. "I'll get you a Moslem sarong and hat, and we'll get dressed up for a costume party — all our own, I hope."

"Now wait just a minute," Jonas protested, concerned that they meant to go alone. "You two have your costume party, but I'm going to be right behind you with my gun, and at the first sign of trouble, you'll hear from me. Is that understood?" His voice was resolute but kind, and Elizabeth knew the others would yield to his wisdom without protest.

Suddenly, loneliness engulfed her again; the two men were quite taken with Maggie. Jonas hadn't even bothered to inquire about her flight, nor did he seem the least bit solicitous about her drenched appearance. Maggie appeared totally wrapped up in her friend's presence, and the smile she had for Jonas was mind-threatening.

"But what am I going to do?" Elizabeth asked in a rush, frowning when her voice cracked with concern. She wanted no one to be aware of her unsettled feelings. Martin's hand covered hers on the table and, feeling the first sting of tears, she drew in a deep breath and turned to face the sympathy in his eyes. Always sensitive to her moods, his perception of her needs was usually comforting and made him a brother to be treasured. But sometimes he knew too much. The saucy grin she gave him didn't quite reach her eyes, but only he would notice that.

"I don't want to be left behind," she said lightly, "while you all are out treasure hunting."

Jonas sighed as though he had anticipated an argument, but he spoke firmly. "Liz, I want you here, where you're safe." As she opened her mouth to protest, he added a gentle, "Please."

Suddenly too tired to argue, and feeling a deep gratitude for the fact that both men were safe, Elizabeth nodded silently and wearily rested her head on a propped-up fist.

She failed to see the smile that lit his face and softened the worry lines around his mouth; it might have relieved her growing jealousy.

Maggie, far younger and prettier than Elizabeth had ever expected, was just the kind of woman Jonas needed. The scene suddenly triggered all of Elizabeth's inadequate feelings from her broken engagement at college, and it seemed only logical that the attention Jonas had given her in Bangkok had come merely from an open, loving personality, not from something deeper as he had said. But all the reasoning in the world failed to relieve her disappointment and pain.

"Come on, Elizabeth," Maggie urged as she stood up. "Let's get you settled in. I wouldn't mind lying down for a little while myself. Jonas, maybe you and Martin could call me in about an . . ."

A sudden explosion outside rocked the house and sent dishes crashing to the floor. "Get down!" Jonas commanded the women. He and Martin dove for a back window and took a cautious look outside. "Something's on fire in the backyard!" Martin yelled, flinging open the back door and rushing out onto the porch.

"It's the servant's house," Maggie called out. "No one is in it now." She grabbed buckets from a work table on her way out the door, thrusting one at each man. "All our water comes from the well. There are two water jars outside. We'll have to do the best we can to keep it from reaching the main house."

"Get the jeep away," Jonas hissed, "before it catches fire and blows up."

Maggie nodded and raced into the house for her keys. The men started to work, using the jar that stood waist-high at the foot of the steps and one that sat on the veranda, and soon the two women were pulling water from the well in the backyard.

Their efforts were like child's play; the fire licked up the water with malevolent glee as it grew stronger. The one-roomed hut was so close to the back steps that sparks were leaping onto the roof of the veranda. Without a miracle the main house would soon catch fire, and then nothing could save it.

As they worked, feverishly throwing water on the back steps and veranda, Elizabeth heard loud voices. A large crowd had gathered to watch.

"Why won't they help?" she asked Maggie as they raced back and forth with buckets sloshing water everywhere.

"You know the Asian mind, Elizabeth. Getting involved with someone else's problem just isn't the thing to do. They aren't cruel; it's not part of their culture."

"I know, but this . . ." Elizabeth just shook her head, took quick aim at the roof, and threw the water as hard as she could.

Martin grunted and turned from the large jar at the steps. "This one's empty. Now what?"

"There's one more," Maggie called out as she tossed the roped bucket down into the deep well and began pulling it back up. "It's in the bathing room."

Jonas and Martin raced in and out of the house, working silently and efficiently, getting what water they could from inside.

The next time Elizabeth returned to the fire from the well, the servant's house was gone, gutted to the ground. Swerving toward the main house with her bucket of water, she gasped. "Look! The veranda roof. It's on fire!"

Martin and Maggie stopped their work and stared upward. Jonas raced out of the house, threw the last bit of water up on the roof, and then dropped the bucket.

"That's the last," he said apologetically. "There's nothing more we can do. Getting it from the well is too slow now; it won't do much good."

"We tried," Maggie said, trying to catch her breath and holding in the tears of frustration. "If only it doesn't spread anywhere else."

Elizabeth understood. Not only were other lives and homes in danger, but Maggie could be shot to death by the police for arson unless the guilty party could be identified.

The fire had now raced across one half of the veranda roof and was reaching up onto the top of the main structure with long, eager arms. In a few moments the whole house would be ablaze.

"All my worldly goods, everything I own, is about to go up in smoke. It's not that I have anything important," Maggie whispered, "it's just that I'll have to start all over. My work, my efforts here, everything."

"Lord," Elizabeth whispered, "please help us now."

"Amen," Jonas added, and Elizabeth felt his hand squeeze her shoulder gently.

And in the next moment, the miracle came.

The sky opened up with such a torrential, pelting rain that it was impossible to see anything. It poured down harder than Elizabeth could ever remember, stinging like ant bites. No fire, no matter how out of control, could live in that cloudburst.

Laughter brought on by relief swept through the crowd of curious neighbors. They had seen enough; now they raced for home and a dry spot. In a moment there were only four people standing in the backyard, thoroughly soaked to the skin, and completely overjoyed.

Maggie wrapped her arms around Elizabeth and began to laugh and cry at the same time. "Thank you, Lord, oh, thank you, Lord!"

In such moments, Elizabeth thought, mankind stands in awe of the direct intervention of God. To say that it was the rainy season and the chances of this happening were substantial was to limit the workmanship of the Creator of this world. It was indeed a miracle!

"Well, girl," Jonas said with a chuckle, "let's go inside and check the damage to your house."

Buckets that moments ago had been used against the fire were soon located in strategic spots under a leaking roof. The kitchen had sustained the most damage, but even the ceiling in the front room had several holes where the rain was pouring in.

Jonas retrieved the jeep and, returning to the front room, pulled back the window curtain and peered out with a thoughtful look.

"What is it?" Maggie asked, holding a stack of papers that she meant to take into her dry bedroom.

"I think you'd better cancel your plans to reclaim the statue tonight, Maggie."

"Why?"

"There's still a crowd standing around outside. We've become the center of attention. You can't leave without being followed."

"Wait until tomorrow night," Martin suggested.

"Maybe," Maggie answered soberly. "A lot of things can happen before tomorrow night."

A soft knock on the front door came like a verbal period to her statement.

"Yes?" Maggie called out.

"Che' Hathway," a man's voice replied, "I have a message for you."

Maggie opened the door cautiously, Jonas and Martin standing right behind her. "Yes, what is it?" she asked the Malay man standing in the darkness.

"You," he said without preamble, pointing to Jonas. "My people want you. Now."

ﻩ   ﻩ   ﻩ

Two men lounging in front of the schoolhouse across the street agreed with Maggie's assessment of the difficulties ahead. Indeed, they had already initiated a few.

Haji Met, the grey-haired leader of the United Moslem
Front, looked at that moment more like a placid old grandfather
than a religious fanatic. He frowned at the house that still
stood — evidence of his thwarted plan.

"*Insha Allah*," he growled, *the will of God,* he thought. But
further activities tonight would also be providential, and in his
favor.

"You know what to do," he said to the younger man standing at his side. "Hasim, I leave it to you."

His son nodded, satisfied that he would now have his way
in the matter. He had been patient; he had dutifully followed
his father's orders long enough. Fingering the knife at his waist,
he spat on the ground with great satisfaction.

"Tonight it will be done," he whispered softly, the cruel
smile on his face a silent, visible warning of his evil heart and a
mind totally committed to his cause, unchangeable.

In a moment the two men were seated in the back of a jeep
and, with a profusion of grinding gears and screeching tires,
sped from the scene of the fire.

C H A P T E R   4

*They took counsel together
against me.*

The Psalmist

I t took the four Americans a few seconds to assimilate this
new threat. Still gripped by the cold horror of the fire and
stunned by the unbelievable relief of the saving downpour, they
stood immobile in Maggie Hathway's front room, their movements arrested by the guttural command from the Malay. Elizabeth, preparing to empty a bucket from under a particularly pro-
ductive leak, froze beside an unscreened, barred window. While
she did not understand his native language, she could understand the man's intentions, even from her position well back in
the room.

Martin leaned against the open door, hands stuffed in the
pockets of his rain-soaked blue jeans, wire-rimmed glasses still
streaked with water. Stiff-backed and resolute, with brown hair
shining in the soft light from the kerosene lamp, Maggie was an
invincible angel staring at the unwelcome visitor. To her left,
Jonas stood astride, arms folded across his chest, every inch of
his tall frame inflexible. His compelling stare prompted the
Malay to fidget uncomfortably. He was simply dressed in a
faded shirt and sarong, and was barefooted. But the unusual scar
that ran across his left cheek and pulled the corner of his eye

down into a distorted stare sent a chill down Elizabeth's spine. She was suddenly very much afraid of the evil she sensed in him.

"Come," the man ordered, motioning toward the street with his chin.

"No!" Maggie resented this intrusion, and stepping forward, launched into a stream of objections, unafraid of resisting this messenger from the illegal Moslem organization.

"*Dak*," she refused once more, speaking in Malay. "My house almost burned down, and I need these men." Waving at the gaping holes in the roof, she demanded, "Can't you see my problem!"

The man was not impressed by that argument, so she dropped the stack of papers from her arms onto a low coffee table and tried again. "No one goes out this late. Come back tomorrow."

But nothing she said changed his mind. The Malay stubbornly confronted each point of contention with a growl and a reiteration of his mission. Finally he had had enough.

"Quiet!" he barked, pulling a gun from the sarong folds at his waist and pointing it at Maggie. "No more talk!"

Undaunted, Maggie opened her mouth to continue her argument.

"Stop!" the man hissed. Maggie prudently obeyed.

Then he spoke directly to Jonas in the Thai language. "What kind of men are you to let this woman speak your words?" Clearly, he expected to skirt the stubborn woman's indomitable force by shaming the foreign men.

"Do you eat rice from a woman's hand?"

Elizabeth shivered, partly from the cold, wet clothes she still had on, and partly from fear that the Malay might win his argument. Knowing that Martin would follow his employer's lead, she turned anxiously toward Jonas, her eyes imploring him not to do anything foolish.

"Jonas," she whispered, "you won't have any protection at night; you'll just disappear and no one will know where you are." But it was clear by the look on his face that Jonas understood the dangers; he had no intentions of being coerced.

"No," he announced firmly, "we will go tomorrow."

"Now!" the Malay insisted. "My orders are to bring you both. I will, if I have to shoot someone." He glanced at Elizabeth and then at Maggie, choosing his target.

Pushing away from the door and stepping in front of Maggie, Martin blocked the man's path. He turned and glanced down at the gun now pointing at his chest. Then, looking straight into the man's eyes, he slowly pulled one hand from his jeans pocket, pushed his glasses back up on his nose, slid his hand back into his pocket, and waited.

This cool reaction pushed the Malay's anger almost to the breaking point, and he turned to Jonas with wild eyes. "I don't care who gets killed," he rasped, "you go with me."

"I think not," Jonas replied softly, attempting to placate the man's unreasonable anger. "Your organization is in desperate need of information. If you harm any of my friends, you'll never find what you want. Now leave this house. I'll meet with your leader tomorrow."

Instantaneously, the man's free hand snaked out around Martin. He grabbed Maggie by the arm and yanked her forward, knocking Martin aside.

Elizabeth gasped and dropped the bucket she had been holding throughout the confrontation, hardly aware of the water splashing over her feet and legs.

The Malay whipped Maggie around in front of his body and pushed the gun against her head. "Now you will listen to me!" Both Jonas and Martin made a move to save her, but they pulled up short at the Malay's warning, "I'll kill her if you try anything!"

No one moved. No one spoke.

The Moslem kept the gun on his hostage, his eyes leaping from one man to the other, waiting for their response. "Now I have the advantage, and by the will of the Prophet Mohammed I will not lose it."

Elizabeth's head pounded with a strong mixture of anger and fear. Maggie's face was calm, but her eyes were riveted on Martin's face.

The gun trembled slightly. It seemed to bring the entire world to a standstill.

Suddenly, a speeding jeep pulled up in front the house. Brakes screeched, the motor cut off, and a deep voice called out in the Thai language, "Miss Hathway, this is the police."

"*Insha Allah,*" the Malay swore, the words rolling out from the back of his throat. He shoved Maggie forward and sprinted to the far side of the front porch.

Martin reached the doorway in time to see him leap over the side into the darkness, then, thinking that they had come to help with this latest attack, he turned to greet the two policemen who climbed out of the jeep. But as they sauntered leisurely up the steps, their manner quite casual, their guns still untouched, Martin felt a wave of unreality sweep over him.

First a bomb, then a house on fire, then the appearance of a fanatic Moslem threatening their lives, and now a neighborly visit by the local police. *What next?* he thought wryly.

What came next certainly wasn't anything he would have expected. A third person behind the police caught his attention. In the darkness, Martin thought it was a woman, but who would be visiting them at night, and why would she be accompanied by the police?

He turned and softly called Maggie's name.

ﯼ ﯼ ﯼ

While the Americans were fighting fires and challenging insurgents, a meeting was being held in a Malay fishing village that hugged the edge of the Gulf of Thailand, two miles from the Pattani airport. The lack of western night life — electricity, cars, city noises — generated the kind of brooding isolation found fifty miles back into the dense jungle.

Most of the twenty stilted huts set in among the coconut trees were shuttered up for the night, a protection against the evil spirits. A few showed the soft gleam of a kerosene lamp. Faint music wafted from the restaurant at the inland edge of the village.

"We must find that statue!" Hasim exploded, staring at his father. "You are Haji Met, our leader. Why haven't you done something before now!" Hasim was the youngest man in the council, yet as the Haji's son, he was the only one who could challenge the leader with impunity.

Haji Met scrutinized the four men who sat cross-legged on woven mats in the house of the village headman. His volatile son, sitting at his right, had an uncanny ability to stir up a riot. Hasim had trained for several years in the Royal Thai Army and had been involved in the clandestine training sessions conducted in the jungle by fanatic elements from other Islamic nations. He had already proven himself in four years of guerrilla warfare, successful ambushes, and the theft of military weapons.

Then there was the school teacher. Rahmad lacked that instinctive ability Hasim had for covert activities, but his eloquence stirred many hearts toward their fight for freedom.

Two more men sat in the circle. One was their host, the village headman, who had provided invaluable resources for the UMF movement. Rahmad had used this man's fishing boat to transport the statue.

The other man, seated on the Haji's left, was a well-known *imam* — a Moslem priest — and owner of a religious school for boys outside Pattani. He had for years used his religious influence to conduct successful propaganda meetings in remote villages, turning his people against the white man's Christian religion. Often his words reminded the young hotheads that their struggle was a religious, not merely a political, battle.

As leaders of the United Moslem Front, the insurgent separatist group in south Thailand, the five men had gathered to await the foreigners' arrival. The low tones of their conversation were punctuated sporadically by angry outbursts from the hotheaded Hasim.

"I *have* done something," Haji Met replied, speaking to his son's complaint as he fingered his prayer beads. The unsteady light from a kerosene lamp in the corner flickered across the deep ridges on his face; a dark evil shifted over skin toughened by years in the sun, hardening the harsh lines around his mouth. Owner of a modest acreage of rubber trees, he was the eldest of the five men. His white, embroidered haji hat signified he had made the sacred pilgrimage to Mecca; but his religious devotion had in no way tempered his devious nature.

The Haji's silence was more to be feared than his son's ranting; he could manipulate and mutilate more lives by his cold, calculating nature than could the gun his son held in such high esteem.

"If you will remember," he went on, "I gave you permission this evening to do what you wish."

"But you've waited too long. You could have taken the Hathway woman days ago. We need that statue."

"We waited for the missing piece," the haji replied. "We cannot sell a damaged statue."

"What do you mean?" his son demanded, anger stirring within him at his father's secrecy. This withheld information was another indication of the Haji's craftiness; he was a sly and dangerous tiger stalking through the night.

"A piece of the statue broke off and was dropped. Our Bangkok agents learned that it was found by the Chinese and brought down here by a foreign woman."

The group burst into questions.

Haji Met raised a hand, and in the sudden silence that followed he warned, "The Chinese want the statue as much as we do. They sent the broken piece to the white woman, and when she arrived on the evening plane today, they stole her suitcase."

"What!" Hasim blurted out. "Did they find anything? Why weren't we there to intercept?"

"We were," his father answered, pointing toward a suitcase half-hidden under a pile of clothes in the corner of the room. He could not be moved by his son's youthful fervor, and after a moment of tense silence, he continued calmly. "The silver wasn't in the case."

"And?" his son prodded.

"And," the Haji added significantly, "their agents will never report to Bangkok." Two dead Chinese meant nothing to him.

To some men the value of human life is minimal; the cause is everything. And since this cause was religious, the life of any infidel wasn't worth much. It wasn't an intentional sadistic cruelty; it was much worse. Haji's fanatical religion warped the mind into a ruthless amorality.

"This should never have happened," Hasim roared. A warning glance from his father softened the tone of his voice, but not his perpetual anger. "Our contact will be here in four days," he protested. "He isn't going to pay for a statue that isn't here." He turned toward the school teacher, furious with Rahmad's failure.

"It wasn't my fault the statue was lost!" Rahmad flashed an annoyed look at his accuser and then turned to the Haji. In his haste to defend his actions, his words tumbled breathlessly out of his mouth. "Just before the Border Police searched the boat, we hid the statue in a bag of rice. They didn't find it, and when we unloaded that night, the bags got mixed up, and the next day the statue showed up at a morning market, and . . ." When he stopped for a breath, his opponent broke in impatiently.

"And it was found by that snooping foreigner!" Hasim's eyes blazed with indignation at such carelessness. He opened his mouth to give Rahmad the reprimand he deserved but was interrupted by his father.

"Enough," Haji Met intoned, privately satisfied with the impassioned emotions swirling around the room. It was his way of controlling people, and he used it to his advantage with chilling dexterity. "We will find the statue."

But Hasim hung on to his dissensions like a dog clings to his bone. Ignoring a warning nudge from the headman, he plunged on. "We need guns. The King will be here in two months for his annual visit to the south. If we're going to kidnap him, we've got to have the weapons. And we can't buy guns without money!"

"We'll have it." His father paused in his habitual fingering of the prayer beads.

"How? You've said yourself that we've taxed the villages about as much as we dare this year. Much more, and we'll have a revolt on our hands."

This reference to the UMF's illegal taxation of the Moslem people in the south brought about a murmur of dissent among the men seated in the circle. Haji Met let the men argue, shrewdly allowing them to express their feelings, knowing it would increase their fanaticism. Listening to a man's arguments increased his sense of self-worth and developed an intoxicating devotion to the Haji himself.

Hearing a cough, Haji Met turned to greet the man ascending the ladder steps into the hut. The others stopped arguing and waited eagerly.

"Well," Hasim barked, "where are they? What have you done with them?"

The man blinked, one lid closing only partially over a drooping eye, and he twisted his neck in an uncomfortable gesture.

"Bring them inside," Hasim insisted, shifting his position to get a clearer look at the silent man. Noting the man's frightened expression, Hasim turned to his father in disgust. One motion of his father's hand silenced his words, and Hasim sat staring at the man, his hand playing with the knife handle at his waist, his longing to deliver a swift punishment almost palpable to the others.

Haji Met pulled thoughtfully at his ear lobe. "You were not successful, eh, Mat'?" he inquired softly.

"*Dak.*"

"First, the snake; now this," Haji Met pointed out.

Mat' waited for permission to explain, not knowing which he feared most—the son's explosive wrath or the father's cool yet cruel penalties for dereliction of duty. Unconsciously he fingered the scar on his cheek. Haji Met eyed the men in the circle around him and jerked his chin toward the door, silently commanding them all to leave.

Three of the men said their farewells and were gone; Hasim remained seated. Haji Met silently contemplated his woven mat as he waited for his son's departure. He did not wish to cause Hasim to lose face by sending him away like a small boy, yet he would not speak until he and Mat' were alone. Finally Hasim rose swiftly to his feet and in a strangled voice said, "Good-night, my father." He moved slowly toward door, the dark threat on his face causing Mat' to step quickly out of his way. Without a backward glance, the son left the hut and climbed down the steps.

Mat' stared down at the floor until the silence began to unnerve him even more. He knew the game the Haji was playing with him, but he couldn't control his fear. Others had crossed this man's wishes and ended up suffering terribly for it — on occasion, to the point of death.

"What happened?" the Haji finally asked, shattering the unnatural stillness into a thousand tiny pieces that tore into Mat's nerves like steel.

"The foreigners refused," Mat' stuttered, the scar on his face turning red. He explained what had taken place at the missionary's house, answering all the Haji's questions. "They will come tomorrow," he finished lamely.

"Listen to me," Haji Met whispered as he rose and stood in front of the hapless man. "You will bring them here tomorrow afternoon, or else." And with that warning, Mat' felt the sharp edge of a knife lying against his cheek. His eyes widened in surprise, for he had not even seen the Haji move his hands, but he stood motionless, waiting to feel a ripping slash across his face.

Haji applied more pressure with the knife.

"You will need to be led about by the hand if you fail. Stake your life on it, Mat'. If you do not bring them here tomorrow, you will never see the sun again. Do I make myself clear?"

"*Yah,*" came the response through lips that barely moved.

Satisfied that Mat' completely understood his position, Haji Met stepped back and motioned toward the door.

"Get out of here," he growled.

*You have made my heart beat
faster with one glance of your
eye.*

Solomon's Love Song

E lizabeth, sit down," Jonas instructed gently. "You look a little washed out." He grinned at her lifted eyebrows and eyed her wet clothes. "No pun intended, but you're shaking." His hand touched the side of her face reassuringly. "Take a deep breath. I'll be back in a minute."

Elizabeth sank down in a high-backed rattan chair. "Where are you going?"

"To make sure our Malay friend hasn't stuck around for another visit," he replied, starting down the hallway that led to the back of the house.

Elizabeth could see Martin and Maggie talking with the police on the front porch. Gratefully, she leaned back in the chair and closed her eyes. But even in this momentary lull, she found it difficult to relax.

How could all this happen in the few hours she had been in south Thailand? Images of the fire and the threats by the Moslems burst across her mind like bolts of lightning, and she wondered what would have happened if the police had not arrived.

It seemed odd that this was the first direct confrontation with the UMF. These men had little compassion toward women and certainly wouldn't hesitate to interrogate a lone foreigner. Why had they not tried to force Maggie to reveal the statue's location before tonight? She alone knew where it was hidden! It was unthinkable to be so suspicious, but the situation did put the missionary in a strange light.

Elizabeth frowned, instantly rejecting such a wild notion. *I'm just too tired,* she reasoned. *How could I ever think of implicating Maggie?*

Jonas had spoken highly of her, a woman who had worked faithfully for the past ten years among the people of southern Thailand. Seeing the physical needs, knowing the spiritual hunger of those who were more ruled by fear of spirits than by a faith in one God, she had worked with love and dedication. How could Elizabeth presume to question her motives?

A voice—Maggie's—called her name, startling Elizabeth out of her curious reflections. Her eyes flew open, and she hoped fervently that her face didn't mirror her thoughts.

"Elizabeth," Maggie said, pushing a few strands of brown hair away from her face, "your new friend is here."

"My . . . ?" Elizabeth asked, and stopped mid-sentence. "Su-Ling!" she exclaimed in surprise, surging to her feet to greet the young woman who had sat beside her on the plane from Bangkok. "Su-Ling, welcome."

"I am sorry to bother you so late." Su-Ling's English was the kind heard only from an Asian, soft with the musical tones and rhythms of her native language. "*Mai pen rai,*" Maggie assured the young woman. "It doesn't matter. You haven't troubled us at all."

Clearly unruffled despite recent events, Maggie graciously invited the young Chinese woman to sit down. At Su-Ling's questioning glance toward the gaping holes in the roof, Maggie explained matter of factly, "The house caught on fire. We were trying to put it out."

Su-Ling's inscrutable look as she listened to Maggie's story left Elizabeth wondering if she already knew about the fire and perhaps even more of the evening's events. She looked every inch the delicate Chinese woman, her immaculate navy skirt and white blouse untouched by the wet weather, her appearance seemingly unaffected by her recent travels.

Elizabeth squirmed inwardly and retreated to her chair. Her drenched hair and bedraggled clothes left her feeling at a distinct disadvantage once again. Why did she have to look like some cleaning woman caught in a rain storm when these two women appeared so elegant?

In a few moments she heard the jeep back out and drive away, and the voices of Martin and Jonas conferring in low tones on the front porch before coming in to meet their guest.

"Su-Ling," Maggie began, motioning toward the men, "this is Elizabeth's brother, Martin. And this is Jonas Adams, who . . ."

"Yes, I know. Jonas Adams of Bangkok." Su-Ling didn't seem surprised to see him.

Elizabeth wondered if the young woman had expected, perhaps even planned, to see Jonas. Then she frowned, angry at her growing suspicion of other people. At this rate, she would soon be questioning her own brother!

Martin took a chair nearby, pulled off his glasses, and searched unsuccessfully through his pockets for a dry handkerchief. "Are you in trouble?" he asked Su-Ling, turning to thank Maggie for the towel she had handed to him. Ignoring Elizabeth's surprised reaction to his uncharacteristic bluntness, he carefully began to wipe one lens and waited. Apparently, Martin's immeasurable patience had worn thin after the day's events, and he had decided to take the offensive.

"T-trouble?" Su-Ling stuttered, her hands fluttering toward the black purse on her lap.

"Yes," Martin smiled. "How can we help you?"

"Oh, I understand." Su-Ling sighed and turned to Maggie, her wide, dark eyes shining in the light. "I cannot find transportation to Yala tonight. My husband has work there." Here she directed her information to Jonas, who leaned against the wall near a window, arms folded over his chest, a lock of black hair slashing down over his forehead.

"My husband is a border policeman." She pulled a picture of a man in uniform from her purse and handed it to Jonas. "I telephoned from the local headquarters, but he is not there. They would not tell me where he is located. I must wait."

Then, shrugging her shoulders, she made a charming appeal to the tall, dark American. "Please, I need help."

In the kerosene lamp's feeble light, Elizabeth couldn't be sure, but she would have wagered a set of dry clothes that the woman had deliberately sent Jonas a provocative look. She wondered if Martin had caught this play for sympathy.

She and Martin were closer than most siblings; they were kindred spirits, easily aware of the other's thoughts and emotions. She suppressed a smile as she heard him murmur, "No doubt about it."

"Pardon?" Maggie asked.

"No doubt about it," Martin repeated, still wiping his glasses. "Miss Su-Ling needs help."

Jonas had seen Elizabeth's reactions and slanted her a warning look. Then, not wanting his longtime friend to feel obligated to keep guests while everything was in such turmoil, he asked, "Maggie, what about a hotel?"

"Oh, no," Maggie objected, turning to Su-Ling. "I couldn't send you back into town. We've plenty of room here. There's an empty bedroom across the hall from Elizabeth. We would be happy to have you stay with us."

"I do not wish to trouble you," Su-Ling offered half-
heartedly.

"It won't be any trouble." Maggie rose to her feet. "Would
you like a cup of hot tea?"

"Yes, thank you," Su-Ling replied. She glanced at Jonas,
still standing near the window. He was well known for his gen-
erosity; but at the moment, he didn't seem to be living up to his
reputation. She hoped she had made a good impression on him.
With these thoughts uppermost in her mind, she started to follow Maggie into the kitchen, forgetting her baggage.

"I'll take this to your room," Martin offered, reaching for
the straw tote bag.

Su-Ling's reaction was instantaneous but a fraction too late.
"No, I'll take it," she argued, frowning as he hooked the bag
straps with two fingers and weighed it in the air for a moment
before surrendering it into her outstretched hand.

"Th-thank you," she stuttered, her eyes darting to
Elizabeth's face and then back to Martin. "I only have this bag
and my purse." She smiled shyly. "I am not accustomed to your
American courtesies."

"Of course, I understand," he responded, returning her
smile and stepping back so that she might follow Maggie. He
sent a curious look toward Jonas before following the two
women out of the room.

Elizabeth left her chair and started toward the doorway. No
matter what new threat might come, she was going to bed.
Jonas was right. She was shaking from exhaustion. But her
steps halted as Jonas turned her around and pulled her close
into a long embrace.

"You're not getting away that fast," he growled in a low
voice.

Elizabeth didn't argue. She felt the strength in his arms and
let her anxieties seep away. She was reluctant to speak, not
wanting to stir up an argument because of her arrival when he

had expressly told her to stay in Bangkok. But after a moment she broke the silence impulsively. "I've never ever had anything like it," she whispered.

"Like what?"

"Your hugs." Her hands rested lightly, timidly, against his back.

He laughed. "Against such a wet shirt, you mean?"

"No," she replied soberly. "Against such caring. I've never had—it's like . . ." She broke off, incapable of putting the feeling into words.

"Well?" he asked gently.

"Well, it makes me feel like I'm the most important person in the world. It's like you're pouring words into your arms—that you care about me."

"I do care, more than you realize."

"No one has ever held me like this."

"Doesn't that say something to you?"

"But what if it doesn't last?"

For a long moment he said nothing. Then he turned his lips against her cheek. "Liz, put your arms around me," he ordered.

After a moment's hesitation, she obeyed.

"That," he sighed, "is like coming home."

"Do you feel it, too?" she whispered in surprise, turning to look up into his face.

"Beautiful blue eyes, so full of questions." He trailed one finger gently across her cheek and then over her lips. "Questions," he repeated thoughtfully, "and chagrin that you spoke so honestly. Am I right?"

Elizabeth pulled away from his arms and sank down into the nearest chair, knowing he could sense her turmoil and feel her racing heart.

"I'm too vulnerable with you," she protested. "I let that happen once before and got hurt. You know that, Jonas. And you know you have the power. . . ."

"Hush," he murmured, leaning over and effectively stopping her protest with a gentle kiss. "Liz, we've gone over this subject before. I can't force your trust, but I want it. More than anything else, I want you to believe in me."

She started to speak, but he stopped her once more; this time the kiss was more urgent.

"I'm not that immature young man who threw you out of his life for a singing career. I'm ten years older than you, and I've had enough experience to know that we can have a deeply satisfying relationship. As a Christian, I'm talking about an honest, caring, loving commitment to each other."

"All right," Elizabeth answered, "you want honesty; so do I. Please, Jonas, don't ever tell me something simply because you think I want to hear it. That's not the kind of affirmation I long for." She looked down at her clenched hands. "Now, I'll be honest. I want to believe you, Jonas, but . . ."

"But, you're going to weigh everything I say and wonder if I really mean it. Right?"

"I'm sorry," she replied, her expression pleading with him. "Can't you understand? I look at you and then at Maggie, and I wonder why you aren't — why you haven't — you two just look like you fit together. I feel like a twelve-year-old school girl, all clumsy and inept."

His eyes were smoldering as he pulled her out of the chair to stand before him, and she wondered if he was angry with her stubbornness. He searched her face intently.

"You're beautiful and charming, and there are many other reasons why I care about you. You're a gentle spirit" — now each word was punctuated with a kiss against the fingers he held — "gifted, intelligent, complex, giving. That young man was blind not to see what he was losing. You've so much depth, Liz. I want to know everything about you; I want to know every facet of Elizabeth Thurston. And I don't mind if it takes a lifetime."

She shook her head, hardly daring to believe what this man was saying. How could he know that her heart longed for such approval?

"No one has ever said those things to me. Ever," she whispered. Her eyes filled with tears and she turned away.

"Don't do that," he whispered. "Don't be ashamed to let me see you cry." One hand tipped her face toward his, the other pulled her close. He kissed away a tear. Then, as he bent to claim her lips once more, she put a hand over his mouth.

"No more." Her voice quivered, but her eyes sparkled. "My legs are so wobbly now I can hardly stand. Any more of this kind of attention and they're going to fold up under me."

"That's what you get for following us down here," he teased.

"And this is my punishment?!" she responded breathlessly.

"We'll talk about that tomorrow, Liz. You're too tired now."

She pushed his arms away and stepped back. "I'm going to bed before I get lost in your words."

The look in his eyes wiped any coherent thought from her mind. For the first time in her life, she experienced the feeling of drowning in the love mirrored in someone's eyes. It wasn't merely a trite expression in a romance novel; it was like bathing in warm sunlight.

But did she dare trust it?

"I love you, Liz. Let it rest," he ordered softly. "Just let it rest."

C H A P T E R   6

They cannot sleep unless they do evil.

The Book of Proverbs

E lizabeth's eyes flew open. Moving her head slightly to the left, she stared out through the mosquito net that surrounded her narrow bed, trying to see into the darkness.

She could not remember being awakened; no one had called her name nor touched her. Nor had she drifted slowly out of sleep. Instead, she had wakened suddenly, her eyes wide open, her heart pounding so hard it seemed to shake the bed. Something had startled her out of a deep sleep; she was positive she had heard a noise. The steady drumming of rain on the roof had started when she first went to bed, and she had fallen asleep under its rhythmic beat. But she didn't think the rain had wakened her.

She wasn't yet familiar with the house, but she remembered that Maggie's room was somewhere near the front and Su-Ling's just across the hall. She had heard them go to bed. She remembered Jonas's gentle assurance that he and Martin would keep guard through the night and his admonition to get a good rest. After that, there had only been the steady beat of the rain.

Perhaps she had been asleep for just a few minutes, but no light shone through the lattice work at the top of the walls. She

lay fully awake, every nerve strained, tentatively, blindly prob-
ing the thick darkness of the room. If only the moon were shining instead of being covered by heavy rain clouds!

Intensely aware of another presence in the room, Elizabeth
felt under the pillow, relieved when her fingers touched the silver belt and the flashlight from Maggie. Her skin crawled with
the knowledge that whoever was in her room might also decide
to search under her pillow.

The flashlight in her hands proved small comfort. If only
she could lift the mosquito net and turn the light on before
being detected, she might have a chance. But just as she
reached for the netting, the chair next to the bed scraped
slightly, paralyzing her. Someone, or something, was right next
to her bed; surely they could hear the thudding of her heart and
realize she was awake.

Although she had no idea what protective measures she
would take once she discovered the intruder's identity, Elizabeth knew she had to so something; the suspense was surely
harder on her nerves than the confrontation. Her imaginative
mind spat out the possibilities with the speed of a computer.
Perhaps it was a small, wild animal, creeping in through the
barred window. Her mosquito net would afford some protection. Or it could be a giant boa constrictor crawling around the
room; her mosquito net would not protect her then. Perhaps the
Malay gunman had returned, strangled Jonas and Martin with
his bare hands, and was now preparing to kill her as well.

The sudden concern for her brother and Jonas galvanized
Elizabeth into action. She jerked the netting up, aimed the flashlight toward the vicinity of the chair, and snapped it on. The
beam of light revealed a sarong-clad figure and a woman's
hand outstretched toward her bed.

Maggie, Elizabeth thought with horror. *Maggie is* involved
and has come to find the silver piece. No wonder she appeared

so calm through all that had happened; no wonder she had
laughed at Jonas's concern for her safety!

These thoughts flashed through Elizabeth's mind in a split
second as the figure stood frozen in the dim light, one hand still
reaching for the mosquito netting. Slowly Elizabeth directed the
light upward—over the sarong and then a white blouse—fully
expecting to see the missionary. She had no idea what she
would say. This was going to be an awkward confrontation.
Jonas would be devastated.

"Su-Ling," Elizabeth exploded. "What are you doing in
here?"

A startled look crossed the Chinese woman's face before
she threw up a hand to shield her eyes from the flashlight's
beam.

"I—I am sorry," Su-Ling whispered. "I got up for a drink
of water. I thought I was in my room. Please forgive me. I am
sorry I disturbed you."

The apology punctured the darkness with staccato-like
sounds as Su-Ling retreated toward the door, and with one last,
"Sorry," she disappeared into the hallway.

Surprised and confused, Elizabeth had not moved during
this exchange, except to follow the retreating figure with the
light. But as soon as Su-Ling disappeared, she sprang from the
bed and ran to the door to peer down the hallway.

Just as she suspected, Su-Ling had not gone directly across
the hall to her room. She was standing at the kitchen door, silhouetted against the low light of a kerosene lamp, conversing
with someone hidden in the shadows. They spoke in low tones;
Elizabeth couldn't hear the words, and it was difficult to distinguish what language they were speaking.

In a moment, Su-Ling turned back down the hall, and disappeared into her room. Elizabeth flattened herself against the
wall to catch sight of who followed. It was Maggie Hathway.

☙   ☙   ☙

Unable to go back to sleep, Elizabeth lay in her bed, pondering Su-Ling's unwarranted appearance. Had she honestly gotten confused about the rooms, or was she hunting for the silver piece? And what part did Maggie Hathway play in all this? No matter how many times she went over all the events, she couldn't find any logical, happy conclusions. But she knew one thing for certain: tomorrow would probably bring even more danger.

With that nagging thought, Elizabeth finally drifted into a fitful sleep, where she dreamed that a mob of dark-skinned children chased her through the jungle, shouting at her in languages she couldn't understand. Behind them marched a swarm of sinister-looking Asian men beating loudly on small drums. The circle of children grew tight around her, and the men came closer. Elizabeth tried to find a way of escape, but there was none. She gasped and jerked away from the clawing hands — and tumbled into consciousness.

The drums of her dream changed into the clattering sounds of someone in the kitchen. She sighed with relief, wondering if Maggie's servant girl was at work or if the others were eating breakfast.

A glance at her watch confirmed the suspicion that she had overslept; it was almost eight o'clock. Usually an early riser, this morning Elizabeth felt drugged, and she struggled to clear fog from her mind. A plane flight, a stolen suitcase, a fire in Maggie's home, a Malay gunman, and eventually, Su-Ling's nocturnal visit. No wonder she still felt exhausted.

Pulling back the mosquito net, she shoved her legs over the edge of the bed and tried to find the energy to get up. On the chair beside the bed lay a white, sleeveless blouse and a brightly flowered, gold-colored sarong. Maggie had remembered Elizabeth's stolen suitcase.

After showering, Elizabeth smiled as she stepped into the sarong; she hadn't worn one for a long time. Pulling it tightly to the right, she folded the extra material across the front into a large pleat and tucked it in securely at the waist. She wore the lightweight cotton blouse out over the sarong for additional comfort.

Pulling a small hairbrush from her purse, Elizabeth made a face in the mirror. Nothing short of a beautician's prowess could control the curl in her soft brown hair during the rainy season. It was just as well that she liked it cut short and had long ago given up fretting over what could not be changed.

"Change," she murmured, thinking of all she had faced in the last month: a broken engagement, her return to Thailand, a kidnapping that almost led to her death, and a deepening relationship with Jonas Adams for which she was unprepared.

Sighing, she turned from the mirror to straighten up the room. She put her sandals on the closet floor, gathered up her clothes to be washed, and, tucking the mosquito net over the headboard, began making the bed. Moving the pillow, she saw the silver belt and flashlight. With a jolt she realized that in all the excitement of the previous evening, she had forgotten to show the silver piece to Jonas!

When the room was straightened to her satisfaction, she took the belt and headed toward the kitchen, enjoying the smooth, clean floor beneath her bare feet. It was one of the advantages of living in Thailand; floors were kept spotless and shoes weren't worn indoors.

She stopped short when she reached the kitchen door, surprised to see Jonas sitting alone at the table. Instead of the immaculate business suit, he wore a pair of blue jeans and a striped cotton shirt. She had never seen him so casually dressed, and it took her a moment to adjust to this new image.

"Good morning," she murmured, happy to see him safe and unharmed. Then, expecting a battle about her arrival, she squared her shoulders and approached the table.

"I've been waiting for you," he said with a loving smile that stopped her again and brought him halfway across the room to meet her. Ignoring the silver belt in her hand, he pulled her into his arms and kissed her eagerly.

When she could speak, she protested. "Jonas, the servants."

"The one servant girl Maggie has is washing clothes beside the well. Relax, I can see her from here," he added, looking through the back window.

"But Maggie and — and Su-Ling?"

"Martin drove them into town. He's going out to the air-port."

"Oh."

"Any other objections, my stubborn American?" His voice was soft and caressing. He kissed her lightly on the temple and then drew back to look into her face. "I can see there are," he said with a knowing smile.

"Are what?" she queried, slightly dazed, but still a little worried. This kind of intimacy between unmarried people was simply not acceptable in Asia. "There are what?" she repeated.

"Objections. What's wrong? Don't you want me to hold you? Don't you like my kisses?"

He was definitely in an amenable mood, Elizabeth thought as she returned his look. "At the moment, they're the best avail-able," she quipped, keeping her face sober.

"Huh," he grunted, the glint in his eye a warning that he intended to show her just how good they were.

Pulling away from him abruptly, she sat down at the table. "I want some breakfast," she said, reaching for a banana.

"Hungry or afraid?" he teased.

"Hungry." Elizabeth tried to ignore the impact he made on her emotions. Ruggedly handsome, he carried his tall frame with ease and purpose as he poured her some coffee.

Well, she thought, *I'm not going to allow another man, no matter how magnetic, to turn my life upside down again.*

"Liz," he warned as he handed her a coffee cup, "stop comparing me to your ex-fiancé."

She looked up, startled, wondering how he knew.

"You get this remote look on your face," he said in answer to her unspoken question. Coming around the table, he pulled out a chair next to her and sat down. "Tell me about it," he suggested gently.

Elizabeth sighed. "He could look at me with a loving expression and tell me that we had a special kind of love and that he had revealed more of himself to me than to anyone else in the world. It was easy for him to speak so openly, but his actions didn't fit his words."

"Are you still bitter?"

Elizabeth frowned with concern. "No, I don't think so. Do I act like it?"

"No," he replied, reaching out to take hold of her hand.

"For a while, the rejection made me feel totally worthless, but I finally gave it all to the Lord and asked Him to bring good out of pain."

"And has He?"

"Yes. I'm just beginning to understand that I am complete and worthwhile as God's child. I know I need to learn that He can take care of my inner needs, instead of depending so much on another human being."

"And can you learn to trust me as well, Liz? I won't let you become too dependent upon me. You have so much to give to the world — gifts and abilities I don't have. Why should I want to stifle all that in your life? I want you to be free to be Elizabeth Thurston." He paused a moment and leaned forward,

"Elizabeth Thurston Adams, that is." He kissed the hand he held and looked intently into her eyes.

Elizabeth was drawn to him. She longed to give in to the romance of the moment and let him kiss away the doubts, yet she knew it was wiser to move cautiously into this new relationship. It took all the strength she could muster to pull her hand from his.

"I'm still hungry," she whispered, unable to turn away from his look.

He smiled and sat back in his chair, freeing her to attend to her breakfast while he went on talking. "Good things do come out of pain," he said almost to himself. "I know it's true. I thought happiness died with my wife, and I steeled my heart against any kind of intimacy. I was afraid that if I loved someone again, I would lose it. No one deliberately sets themselves up to be hurt."

Elizabeth reacted involuntarily to his words, reaching out to touch his hand. "I'm sorry. I can't imagine what it's like to be widowed."

"I went through life like a robot. I was miserable. It took me a couple of years to realize that to be a growing Christian, I had to love. It's the only way. And to love is to be vulnerable, even to pain."

Elizabeth felt a sense of awe creep into her heart as she listened to such honesty. *This man,* she thought, *knows more about the business of life than I ever will.* A new thought came to her mind as she searched his face, absorbing what she had just heard.

"Jonas, may I ask you a question?"

"Sure."

"If you care for me," she asked, "why were you so cool when I arrived last night? You had more interest in Maggie than in me."

He pushed back the lock of dark hair from his forehead with a touch of frustration. "Liz, this situation is very dangerous. I don't want to lose you, too. I wanted you in Bangkok, where you'd be safe."

"But what makes you think I want to be there when you and Martin are here?"

"Is that why you came?"

"Partly," she replied, pushing her belt across the table. "Remember that I mentioned receiving a silver piece?"

"It's in here?" he asked, picking up the belt. "Clever idea. No one could tell you're wearing a piece of royal antiquity. I suspect someone planned to put this back on the statue before selling it, and you were a safe courier. You can be sure they're going to come looking for it now."

"Then it will be safe just where it is. I'll keep wearing it, and no one will be the wiser."

Jonas frowned and shook his head, pushing his hand through his hair once more. "I don't like it."

"Jonas, you just said the entire situation is dangerous. It can't be any worse if I wear the belt like it is. This way, we'll know just where the piece is if we need it. Besides . . ." She stopped, remembering Su-Ling's visit.

"Besides what?"

"Oh, nothing." She felt silly accusing someone of searching her room when Su-Ling's explanation seemed so reasonable. She would just keep that suspicion to herself and watch for clues from both the women.

"Tell me, Liz."

"Well," her thoughts went to something more serious, "you and Martin are going to be in more trouble if you contact the UMF leaders. I'm afraid. I wish you wouldn't go."

"I don't think we'll have much choice. If we can't leave town until we have the statue, we're going to have a confrontation, whether we want to or not. But I've taken a few expedient measures just in case we need help."

Suddenly Elizabeth's appetite was gone; she wasn't hungry anymore.

CHAPTER 7

*How my adversaries have
increased! Many are rising up
against me.*

The Psalmist

Maggie shared her three-fold plan with Martin and Su-Ling on the way into town that morning. "First, I have to report the fire to the police, and then I must find some workmen who will repair the roof immediately."

The third reason she kept to herself. She wanted some time alone with Su-Ling — a few unobserved moments to come to an understanding with this new guest. It wasn't mere coincidence that the girl had appeared at her doorstep, and something about her manner bothered Maggie. It would be good to clear the air and find out just what Su-Ling's mission was without involving Martin or Jonas.

"Going to take time at the station," Martin warned, steering the jeep around a group of children on their way to school. "Asian bureaucracy can't be hurried. Even the police."

"I've had the impression that you have a patient, easy-going nature," Maggie replied. "I'm surprised you're concerned about time."

"Don't mind the wait," he assured her with a lazy smile, "and I'll admit I'm phlegmatic. Watching people and events is fascinating and highly educational."

"You will fit in well with the Asian mind, Mr. Thurston," Su-Ling offered from the back seat.

Martin laughed. "Thanks for the compliment. But Maggie, I have a feeling you're in a hurry."

Maggie glanced at his face, wondering if he had sensed her desire to talk with Su-Ling, and she worried that he would try to get involved. "I'm just concerned that it will take hours to find workers, haggle over prices, and then get them to agree to come today."

"Today?" Martin asked. "But with what's happened with the . . ." He was about to mention the statue when Maggie stopped his protest with a warning glance. He changed the subject smoothly. "With the fire, don't you think the police will insist you wait until they investigate?"

"I hope not," Maggie flared. "I intend to have the repairs done immediately. I won't have everything in my home spoiled by the rains."

Martin said nothing, but he grinned at her spirit.

"I will find the workmen for you," Su-Ling suggested. Against Maggie's grateful refusal, she insisted. "But I can get Chinese men, and I won't allow them to charge high prices. Please, it will be a small thing I can do in return for your kindness to me."

Martin glanced over his shoulder as he drove. "You're a stranger here. How can you find them?"

Su-Ling smiled. "Every Chinese in Pattani will know the best workers. I only need to ask. And I will not let them take advantage of me." When Maggie hesitantly agreed, Su-Ling turned to Martin. "Would you like to come with me while Miss Hathway is at the police station?"

"Ah, no thanks," Martin replied after a second's hesitation. "I'm sure you can find men. I'll stick with Maggie. In case there are problems."

"It would save time if you dropped us off at the station," Maggie suggested. "Su-Ling can look for workers, I'll take care of things with the police, and you can drive out to check the plane. I know you're concerned about it."

"Good idea, but I want you to see the plane, Maggie. I'll just stick with you."

Martin didn't mention the agreement he and Jonas had made the night before. Until they got her safely back to Bangkok, Maggie Hathway wouldn't go anywhere alone. He would have liked to keep an eye on Su-Ling, but protecting Maggie had priority over any curiosities he had developed.

Maggie looked at the man next to her with new interest, suddenly sensing a stubborn streak below the quiet spirit he displayed and, realizing the matter was settled, offered no resistance to his plan.

ɛ ɛ ɛ

Maggie was not accused of setting fire to her own home, but it did take the police over two hours to make a leisurely investigation of the details, filling out form after form. Martin sat patiently through it all, occasionally banking the impatient fire he saw in Maggie's eyes with an encouraging smile. Later outside the police station Maggie sputtered, "You, Martin Thurston, are the epitome of politeness! Are you sure you don't have some Asian blood in you somewhere?"

He grinned and settled his glasses more firmly on his face. "Don't think so. Surprised at you, though. You know that the more you try to hurry people, the more pedantic they become."

"I know," Maggie sighed. "I've just let the situation get to me. I'm not usually this agitated."

"Maggie," Martin chuckled, "you're a tornado on two legs. Have a feeling that you can stir up a lot of turbulence when you're on a crusade. Might be interesting to stick around and find out."

Maggie's startled look killed the gleam of protest in her dark brown eyes as she scrutinized his face. "Is that some kind of proposal of interest in me?" she asked with typical frankness.

"Yes. Do you object?"

"I'm not sure," she confessed. "Why would you be interested?"

"Why not? Come to south Thailand expecting to see a woman worn out from ten years of work in a difficult environment. Thought you'd need a shopping spree and a visit to the beauty shop. What did I find? A gorgeous gal who looks more like someone off a magazine cover than a missionary." He ignored her frown of protest and went on. "*And*, I'm attracted to her inner beauty. Her spirited nature is intriguing."

"For the first time in my life, I'm speechless," Maggie conceded.

"Great," Martin teased. "We're making progress."

"Martin Thurston," she hissed, "if Su-Ling weren't arriving right now, I'd give you a piece of my mind!"

"Looking forward to it," Martin drawled as they turned to greet the Chinese woman.

Su-Ling had found men who were willing to go to work immediately, and she insisted on taking a pedicab to the house. She would explain everything to Jonas, and he could conclude the bargaining for the work involved. It would all be taken care of without Maggie having to get involved.

Reluctantly, Maggie agreed, remembering she still needed to stop at the morning market—one of her daily chores, since her refrigerator always warmed up during the hottest part of the day.

After putting Su-Ling in a pedicab and watching the driver
pedal slowly off toward the outskirts of town, Martin drove to
the shops and parked the jeep in front of the market area — a
block-wide, tin-covered, open pavilion with rows of wooden
counters replete with all kinds of merchandise. He followed
Maggie down one row filled with Swiss fabric, razors, transis-
tor radios, Chinese umbrellas, Thai silver, and toys from Japan.
"Stop stewing about it," he said as they inched their way
through the crowd.

"About what?" she asked over her shoulder.

"About accepting help. You're as independent as my sister.
Maybe worse."

"I think I've managed quite well," she retorted.

They made their way past the fruit stalls: fresh bananas, cus-
tard apples, pineapples, rambutans, and the odorous jackfruit.
The smell of dried fish, curry, and other spices coming from
neighboring booths was mouth-watering.

Followed by a mob of noisy children, they came to the
meat stalls located at the back of the market. It was morning,
and what little fresh meat left was covered with flies.

"I think I'll get a chicken," Maggie said pragmatically after
casting a doleful eye over the possibilities. "My servant girl
doesn't mind killing and dressing one."

"What is wrong, foreigner?" a harsh, accented voice ques-
tioned from nearby. "Are you too good for the meats offered
here?"

Martin turned to see that they were surrounded by Malay
men who stared at them with cold, unfriendly eyes. This wasn't
the usual curious, friendly crowd who enjoyed making light-
hearted fun of the strange things the foreigner did; these men
were hostile.

The man who had spoken to Maggie was the leader. It
wasn't just his western clothes that set him apart; there was
something magnetic about the man that held the crowd spell-

bound. If he chose to have the foreigners beaten to death on the spot, it would happen. And he was aware of his power; he smiled at Martin's silent appraisal of his authority.

Maggie whipped around to confront the man. "You aren't Malay, are you?" she asked, ignoring his attempt at intimidation.

"No, I am from the Near East." He threw back his head with pride and sneered, "My name is Ahzid. I am here to . . ."

"I know why you're here," she interrupted. "You're here to stir up trouble for the Moslems."

Ahzid's face grew dark, and through thin lips he hissed, "You are the ones in trouble. I have only to snap my fingers and you will be dead. Would you like to challenge me?"

"You're too eager," Martin responded, drawing closer to Maggie, refraining from putting a protective arm about her only because of the eastern attitude toward public displays of affection.

Clearly wanting to incite the crowd, Ahzid began to rant at the two Americans, his tirade filled with hatred. "You don't belong here. You are lackeys for the Thai government, helping them keep our Moslem people in slavery. You pretend to be religious, but you come to take all you can from the poor. Mohammed is our prophet; we don't need another!"

As he turned to the crowd, haltingly repeating his speech in their language, Martin whispered, "Come on, Maggie, it's time to leave." He stepped behind her, and they moved toward the edge of the crowd.

Disinterested in a woman, the men let Maggie pass through the circle but closed in on Martin, their growls of protest and hatred growing louder and louder. He tried to push forward, but they stood their ground. He saw Maggie begging several spectators for help, but they turned their backs on her; they were afraid of getting in trouble with local authorities.

Angry men began shoving Martin back and forth across the circle. He knew he had to do something fast or be thrown to the floor and trampled to death.

He side-stepped the next pair of hands and tried to force his way through, but the minute he touched a man, a smoldering hatred broke loose. He was picked up and thrown against a stall. The impact slammed the breath out of his body, sending his glasses flying off his face to the floor, where Ahzid's well-shod foot ground them to pieces. He tried to grasp the railing and pull himself to his feet, but once again was lifted, punched in the stomach with a driving blow, and thrown into the side of another stall.

Blood trickled down his forehead, and he knew that without help there was no way he would survive this assault. The thought of leaving Maggie unprotected stayed uppermost in his mind, driving him to stagger to his feet again and again.

Finally, the shouts of the crowd grew dim, replaced by a roaring in his head that silenced all other noises — a prelude to unconsciousness. He leaned against a post, the world spinning crazily about him, his strength almost gone. A bizarre clanging noise he could not identify mixed with the roaring sound in his ears.

Two police jeeps raced around the corner, their high-pitched sirens scattering the crowd like birds frightened by gunshot. As the police screeched to a halt, Martin could hear the confused shouts of his retreating adversaries.

Malays rushed past. One man gripped a knife low at his side, intending to kill the foreigner who waited helplessly in his path. Martin blinked his eyes to clear his mind, saw the knife, and commanded his body to get away from the danger. But his body refused to respond. At the last second he lunged to one side with herculean effort, trying to escape and yet expecting to feel the weapon. Searing pain shot through him as the knife slashed across his arm.

A peculiar silence filtered slowly into his awareness as he stood slumped against a stall, and he looked up to find the police, merchants, shoppers — everyone — gaping at the spot he had just vacated. Following their stares, Martin saw the knife, half of its blade plunged into the wooden post, quivering with the impact.

ᴈ   ᴈ   ᴈ

Su-Ling arrived back at Maggie Hathway's house about fifteen minutes before the workers arrived. She found Jonas standing on the back porch railing trying to assess the damages on the roof, and she waited at the bottom of the steps until he had turned in her direction.

"Excuse, please," she said softly, "I have returned."

"Yes, I see," Jonas replied, jumping down from the railing. He met her at the top of the steps. "Where are Maggie and Martin?"

"They went to the market," Su-Ling replied, continuing her explanation. "I wanted to help Miss Hathway and have found workers to repair the roof. I hope it is a fair price. I told them you would make the final agreement." She bowed her head modestly and murmured, "I leave it to you, Jonas Adams."

"Thank you, Su-Ling. You've accomplished a great deal, getting a work crew so quickly. I'm sure Maggie appreciates your help."

"It is so little for her kindness to me."

Just then a flatbed truck carrying lumber and about six men pulled into the driveway, and the driver hopped out to inspect the roof. "I'll check it out with them," Jonas said, giving her no indication of his personal approval.

Su-Ling watched from the porch while the two men went through final negotiations. The American's language ability and his business acumen impressed her, and she saw from the Chinese foreman's reaction that no one could take advantage of this foreigner. They completed the deal quickly, and soon men were up on the roof, clearing away the burned tiles and measuring beams that needed replacing.

Su-Ling went to her room with a satisfied smile on her face. Jonas Adams had spoken of her accomplishment. She was amused that she had attained more than he could ever have imagined. The opportunity to find the workers had also given her a natural opening to meet her contact in the city. Unable to have more than a moment alone with him, she had identified herself and asked him to join the work crew. There he was now, and from her window she could see him tossing the old tiles into a large basket. He must have felt her gaze, for after hoisting the basket up onto the back of the truck, he stopped to wipe the perspiration from his forehead and turned to look directly into her window.

They had agreed to meet as soon as possible so that she might relay instructions from their Bangkok superiors, and he had a great deal of information critical to the completion of her mission. She would be on guard for an appropriate moment.

C H A P T E R   8

God has spoken unto us
by His Son.

The Book of Hebrews

L unch time had come and gone, and Maggie and Martin
still had not returned from town. Elizabeth simply could
not shake the feeling that something dreadful had happened. In
the fifteen hours since the plane had landed at the Pattani airport, it seemed as though the problems had piled up, one after
another, like wool blankets in summer.

If Jonas felt any concern, he hid it well. Elizabeth had been
grateful for his prayer before lunch; it had come from a faith
that was calm and encouraging. He had done his best to keep
her mind on other things while they ate, prompting Su-Ling to
talk about Bangkok and sharing some of his experiences while
traveling the country looking for export items.

"I once ran into a smuggling ring up country in the hills.
They were ready to throw me into the river because they
thought I was a competitor, but I managed to convince them
that I was harmless."

The stricken look on Elizabeth's face brought his story to
an abrupt halt, and he spoke to her reassuringly. "They'll be
home soon, Liz. Don't be troubled."

But troubled she was, and with ample reason she thought. The very fact that there had been so many attacks — snakes, fires, guns, assailants, threats — only made an assault on the street or even a kidnapping seem highly possible.

Increasingly uneasy, Elizabeth wandered through the house after lunch: from the front veranda, to the living room, down the main hall, and past the bedrooms to the kitchen where she tried to stand at the table and sketch, but the hanging plants on the veranda that were bursting with fuchsia and scarlet blossoms brought her no joy; the pictures on the living room wall, intricately created from Thai silver, drew no more than a glance; and the children playing in the school yard across the street seemed light years away. Peering expectantly through the nearest window each time she heard a car on the street, Elizabeth was thankful that Jonas was supervising the work on the roof. She would not have been able to maintain her thin facade of calmness. Perversely, the conviction grew in her mind that something was wrong; something had happened to Martin.

She found Su-Ling kneeling beside a large wash basin on the back porch, scrubbing the clothes she had worn the day before. "It's hard to dry things in the rainy season, isn't it?"

The woman paused in her work and nodded toward the porch railing. "Yes, but I hang them there."

"Su-Ling, did Miss Hathway have any other errands to do before coming home?"

"Errands?" Su-Ling asked in a soft voice, each "r" typically blurred. "I do not understand."

"Task, work. Did she plan to go other places after the market?"

"Ah." Understanding lit the almond-shaped eyes. "No, I do not think so. She only talked about going to the market. Perhaps the jeep will not work." Her expression was enigmatic as she looked up at Elizabeth. "You are troubled?"

"Yes, a little."

"Do you think they are in danger?"

"I don't know." Elizabeth turned away from those piercing eyes and sat down on the top step of the porch. Something harsh in Su-Ling's nature lay hidden under that inscrutable look she wore. "I just feel there is a problem."

Su-Ling went back to her work, her eyes returning to Elizabeth several times as she scrubbed and rinsed the clothes. Finally, she ventured, "They will come soon. People here do not have hurry spirits like you Americans."

Elizabeth smiled. "Yes, I know," she sighed. "Sometimes we need more trust and less worry."

Su-Ling shrugged her shoulders. "I do not believe we can change our fate, so I do not worry."

"Is fate . . ." Elizabeth hesitated, trying to think of a synonym for the word *capricious* that Su-Ling would understand. "Does fate change on a whim? Is it cruel one time, kind the next?"

"Yes," nodded Su-Ling. "Yes, it is like the wind. Sometimes gentle, sometimes monsoon."

"Can you trust fate?"

"No," the woman replied bitterly.

"Why not?"

Su-Ling stood up and silently began to drape her clothes over the porch railing, pondering the question. She did not answer until she had hung the last piece.

"Fate is chance. It—it has no heart."

Elizabeth nodded. "Yes, you're right."

Defiance flashed across Su-Ling's face as she tipped the wash basin over the side of the porch, then took a dipper of water to rinse it out. Her next question mocked Elizabeth a little. "Does your God have a heart?"

"Oh, yes." Elizabeth's smile was genuine. "Yes, He does."

"How do you know this?"

"I know He has a heart and that He loves because He died for us."

Su-Ling shrugged her shoulders. "Then your God is dead, like the wooden gods my mother worships." Her words were full of irony.

"No, He came back to life. He lives again, and He has power to take care of me, and you."

Su-Ling's face clouded with suspicion, but she sat down beside Elizabeth. "How do you know this God is alive?" she challenged. "Have you seen Him?"

"Not with my eyes, but with my heart. Do you understand that?"

Su-Ling nodded. "Yes, Orientals see with their heart, perhaps more than the *farang* does. But how can you be sure that what you see with your heart is true?"

"That's a good question." Elizabeth paused, wanting to be sure that she expressed her thoughts in simple enough English for Su-Ling to understand. "Su-Ling, if a man died, was put in a grave, and then came back to life three days later, would you believe his words?"

Su-Ling looked at the American in disbelief. That sounded too simple; surely these were deceitful words. "Did others see him die?"

"Oh, yes. People nailed Him to a tree and watched him die."

"Ah, but did anyone see him alive after the three days?"

"Yes, many people did. Tell me, Su-Ling, would you believe the words of someone like that?"

Grudgingly the woman admitted, "Yes, I suppose I would."

"Well," Elizabeth said, "I can trust what I see with my heart because my God did that, and He left His words for me to read. Would you like to see them, in your own language?"

"Perhaps," Su-Ling shrugged. "I have already heard the mission people in Bangkok speak about their holy book." Then ap-

parently enjoying Elizabeth's original concern, she smiled
slightly and asked, "Do you think your brother is in danger?"

"Yes, I feel he is," Elizabeth replied honestly. "But, Su-
Ling, there is a deeper danger."

Su-Ling frowned. "What do you mean? Deeper?"

"Do you believe that your soul will live forever?"

"Perhaps," the Chinese girl replied.

"Then, is it not far more dangerous if your soul does not
have peace with God? The body may die, but our spirits live on
and . . ."

"*I* am not Christian! Excuse, please, I have work I must
do," Su-Ling exclaimed, interrupting Elizabeth's explanation.
Clearly, she did not wish to hear anything more.

Suddenly, a rain shower stopped their conversation. Su-
Ling ran to pull her clothes from the railing, and Elizabeth went
to look out the front window, hoping she would see the jeep returning from town.

The rain drove the repairmen to shelter, one of them walking with Jonas to the back porch while the others squatted in
Chinese fashion on the front veranda. Seeing Elizabeth's concerned expression, Jonas propelled her toward the kitchen table
and gently demanded that she finish her sketching.

"I can't," she sighed. "I'm not in the mood; I just can't
keep my mind on it."

"Sketch the two Chinese men on the airplane," he instructed. "Force your mind to think about them again. What did
they look like? The shape of the head? The haircut? Any scars
or blemishes?"

With a sigh she tried to concentrate, her hand moving hesitantly over the paper, lightly tracing two portraits.

"It's no use," she complained, gesturing toward the paper.
"They had no special features that I can remember. I wouldn't
even recognize them if I passed them on the street."

"Then sketch your parents," he persisted. "After all, it's important for me to know them. I want their approval." He crossed the room to the stove. "I'll get us something to drink. Ice cubes and cold drinks aren't popular commodities here. Will you settle for hot tea?"

"Yes, thanks," Elizabeth murmured, trying to focus her thoughts on her parents, letting the techniques of art settle her mind, as it so often did. "You know, don't you, that sketching is therapeutic for me?"

"I thought it might help." He turned to look at her from across the room. "And you shouldn't feel guilty about it."

Her hand was arrested momentarily. "What do you mean?"

"I think you feel a little guilty sometimes about enjoying your creative gifts, and you shouldn't. They're God-given, and I think He is pleased when our gifts bring us happiness. After all, we're His children; He said that He had come to bring us joy." Jonas filled the tea kettle and lit the kerosene stove. "You use your art in worship, don't you?"

"Yes, I like to sketch the things I want to pray about. But how did you know?"

"Remember, I saw the sketches you did while you and Martin were hiding at my house in Bangkok. Liz, what's the difference if we sing a hymn, listen to music, write a poem, or meditate in order to get rid of the clutter in our lives so that we can hear God speak to us?"

He foraged through the cupboards, found the tea box and two cups, then turned to find her watching him. "What's the smile for?"

"You amaze me. You're perceptive and . . . and . . . sensitive. You aren't uncomfortable with tears, and you don't condemn weaknesses. I've never met a man so open and accepting."

"What have I got to lose, except what's most valuable — intimacy, love?"

She looked up into his face as he leaned over the table. "And you're willing to be that exposed?"

"No one ever finds love, the really deep kind, without being vulnerable."

She stared into his eyes and shook her head. "What's wrong?" he asked softly.

"I don't know why you would want me," she whispered.

His dark eyes were intensely serious. "It's easy to love someone like you, Elizabeth Thurston."

Impulsively she reached up to touch his face, letting her caress speak the words she could not yet utter, knowing her heart was in her eyes. For a long moment they were content just to enjoy the look they shared, savoring the joy of a growing affection.

A car door slammed shut, breaking into their private world, shattering the intimacy of their discovery. Reluctantly, Jonas broke away and glanced out the window. "They're here," he said, then drew in his breath.

"What's wrong, Jonas? What is it?"

"Maggie's driving, and it looks as though Martin's been hurt."

Martin negotiated the back steps without help, then leaned against the railing to catch his breath. "Sorry, Sis," he mumbled to Elizabeth, "I hope we haven't frightened you."

"I'm just thankful to see you in one piece," she murmured gently, taking in his dirty, torn clothes and his bruised face. "Where are your glasses?"

"Smashed to bits. There's another pair in my suitcase."

"I'll get them," she replied, relief at seeing him alive causing her turn to the mundane. "You'd better sit down before you fall."

Jonas stepped aside, watching Martin's cautious and halting steps into the kitchen, waiting to speak until they were away

from the Chinese worker and Su-Ling, who had been visiting
on the porch until the rain slacked off.

Once inside, he turned to Maggie and asked quietly, "What
happened?"

"A riot."

"About the statue?"

"No, I don't think so. A Moslem missionary from a Near
Eastern country incited a mob of men at the market."

"They were concerned only with Martin?"

"Yes," Maggie admitted ruefully, "they let me go but
started throwing him around. And, of course, no one wanted to
help. When the police finally arrived, the crowd ran for cover,
but one man tried to stab Martin before getting away."

Jonas turned to Martin. "Are you all right?"

Martin sank down in a chair beside the table and nodded.

Maggie resumed her story. "The police went tearing off
after the rioters. We went to the hospital but had a long wait.
The wound is deep; he has a lot of stitches."

Elizabeth returned to the kitchen in time to hear the last of
Maggie's explanation. She helped Martin put his glasses on and
then stood at his side, her arm around his shoulder. "What re-
course do we have against the men who did this?" she asked.

"Not much, I'm afraid," Maggie admitted. "It's too bad that
a few people have to spoil the reputation of others who are gen-
uinely open and kind toward us. We've been warned to expect
something." Then she started issuing orders.

"Martin, go to bed. Wounds don't heal easily in the tropics;
you'll have to be careful of infection. Jonas, help him. The medication should help him sleep for awhile. Elizabeth, he ought to
have something to drink — milk, or some of that tea. I'll go
make some explanation to Su-Ling. I'm sure she's curious."

Elizabeth was stunned. Who did Maggie Hathway think she
was! She had probably instigated the whole thing herself. After
all, she hadn't even been touched. That's why she was showing

about as much emotion as a Buddhist priest in a trance. While
Elizabeth poured milk into a glass, an inner storm brewed. Had
Maggie walked into the room just then, she would have
touched off an explosion. She was still sputtering when she
took the milk in to Martin.

"Some missionary! Has she got a heart at all? She's acting
like you just stubbed your toe at a picnic. I can't believe it!"

Martin was sitting on the side of his bed, his arm outstretched while Jonas eased his shirt sleeve over the wound. He
grinned weakly at his sister's outburst.

"She's concerned," he answered after drinking the milk.
"Being on her own for ten years, she's learned to be strong and
take charge, no matter how badly she feels." He sank back on
the bed and closed his eyes.

"You should have seen her after the riot was over, she, ssh-
hee . . ." Unable to finish his sentence, he waved a hand in
resignation, sighed deeply, and succumbed to the medication.

Jonas motioned for Elizabeth to leave the room, and stepping into the hall after her, murmured, "He'll feel better after a
sleep."

"What are we going to do, Jonas? We need to get away
from here before something terrible happens. Can't we just take
Maggie to Bangkok and then tell the authorities where to find
the statue?"

Jonas shook his head. "Yes, if we could talk Maggie into it,
but now she doesn't want to move Martin."

Maggie's blasé attitude was making Elizabeth furious.
"Well, Jonas Adams," she sputtered, "if you don't do something, you'll be next!"

Jonas saw the tears brimming in her eyes and pulled her
into his arms. "Thank you," he murmured, "for your concern."
His lingering kiss made her feel weak all over, but it couldn't
erase the fear in her heart.

C H A P T E R 9

*Treasures of darkness, riches
stored in secret places.*

The Prophet Isaiah

C he' Hathway! *Sakit-lah!*" a high-pitched voice shouted
from the front yard. It startled the men on the roof and
brought Elizabeth to the veranda.

A thin, dark-skinned Malay woman in a flowered maroon
sarong and white blouse slipped out of her wooden clogs, hast-
ily splashed water over her feet, and mounted the steps, still
calling loudly for Che' Hathway. Nervously tucking a few
strands of coal black hair into the bun at the nap of her neck,
her unintelligible words cascaded over Elizabeth like rain off
the roof.

Her voice ricocheted through the house, breaking into
Maggie's earnest conversation with Su-Ling on the back porch,
and the missionary hurried to the front door.

Ignoring the workmen, whose inborn curiosity had pulled
them around to the veranda, the visitor burst into a barrage of
Malay the moment Maggie appeared. Her appeal was replete
with the word *sakit,* which Elizabeth understood to mean sick-
ness. Several times the woman glanced anxiously toward two
men waiting in a jeep parked in front of the house.

Finally, Maggie interrupted, questioning the woman in her own language, and then explained to Elizabeth. "I know this woman; she's from Golok Village, about five miles east of here. She says her little boy is very sick, and she wants me to take him to the mission hospital. It sounds like pneumonia. Probably near death. They wait too long before getting medical help."

Elizabeth eyed the woman and the two men in the jeep. "How do you know her story is true? Suppose this is a trick?"

"It may be," Maggie murmured, "but I can't take the chance. If she's speaking the truth and I don't help, I'll never get her trust again. The Moslem community would laugh me out of the country. My ministry would be ruined."

After reassuring the woman once more that she would help, Maggie answered Elizabeth's concerned frown with an unequivocal, "I have to go," and then strode into the house.

Jonas was standing in the living room, hands on his hips. "I'm going with you," he announced.

"It's not necessary," Maggie assured him with typical independence.

"You know very well this could be a trick, Maggie. Now use your head," Jonas growled. "We had an invitation at gun point last night from the UMF; they're going to follow through on that. I've been waiting for something like this all day. And you will *not* go by yourself."

The two friends glared at one another for a moment, then Maggie gave in with a chuckle. "I've never won an argument with you yet, Jonas Adams."

"Well, it isn't because you haven't tried!"

"I'd like to know how you get away with it, Elizabeth." The amusement in Maggie's voice softened her words. "I've seldom changed this man's mind!" She hurried through the living room, throwing words back over her shoulder as she went. "Jonas, get your shoes on if you're going with me. I'll get my medicine kit and a flashlight. Elizabeth, if you need the jeep, the keys are in the desk in my room."

The sound of drum beats from the nearby mosque cut through Maggie's next words. "Five times a day, the faithful are called to prayer, but I suppose our friends in the jeep have something more urgent on their minds than that drum," she observed as she left through the front door.

Jonas's last words were sobering. "If this turns out like I think it will, you'll probably get a ransom note: two people in exchange for a statue. Martin has information on the UMF leader, his village, and some places where they might take hostages. He probably won't get much assistance from the police, since they don't want to stir up an international incident, but I talked with the Chinese pastor in town, and he offered to help in any way he can. Go see him if you need to. And, Elizabeth," he concluded as he gave her a quick hug, "I love you. Trust my heart."

His reassuring smile had little affect on her sense of inadequacy, but the moment he left the house, she darted into Maggie's room, grabbed the keys from the desk drawer, and ran to the veranda. At the top of the steps, Su-Ling grasped her arm and refused to let her leave the house.

"You cannot follow," she warned, her precise English grating on Elizabeth's sense of urgency. "They will see you. I have a friend to do it."

"What do you mean?" Elizabeth demanded.

Su-Ling stepped over to the railing and gave a sharp command in Chinese. The man she had been talking with on the back porch nodded, spoke to the foreman, and then sprinted to the truck. The engine sputtered, and the gears ground out a greaseless protest as he backed out of the yard. The motor coughed, stuttered, and jerked its way down the road, then picked up speed, and in a moment, was gone.

Elizabeth whirled around to face Su-Ling. "I want an explanation," she sputtered. "Why did you tell that worker to go after them? Why are you getting involved? What do you know about the —"

"The silver statue?" Su-Ling suggested softly. She motioned toward the living room. "Go inside, away from the others. I do not want to be heard."

Elizabeth glanced once more down the road that was now empty of jeeps and trucks, and reluctantly went inside. The last thing she wanted to do right then was spend time in a long, cozy conversation with a woman she hardly knew. Yet, she had to admit that it would be wise to hear what Su-Ling had to say.

"Well," she asked impatiently as she sat down in one of the rattan chairs, "What do you have to tell me?"

Su-Ling stared at her for a moment and then began to talk, her voice so low that Elizabeth had to lean forward to understand her accent.

"I am instructed from certain authorities in Bangkok to come here. I am to find the statue."

"What statue are you talking about?" Elizabeth folded her arms, unconsciously protecting the silver piece in the belt tucked under the sarong folds at her waist.

"I am talking about the old statue taken from the royal museum — the one Miss Hathway found."

"Who do you work for?" Elizabeth asked suspiciously, toying with the jeep keys still in her hand.

"I am employed by people who do not wish to be identified. I am to return the statue at once." Su-Ling's gaze had not faltered, nor had she reassured Elizabeth. "I do not have identification. That would be dangerous; I could be killed. You must trust me."

The two women assessed each other as they thought of the information they both harbored; one cautiously moving forward in her plan, the other wisely backing away for reflection.

"If you are some sort of agent," Elizabeth demanded, "why were you so shy on the plane? Why did you pretend to be so helpless?"

"What would you have done if I had told you of my mission?"

Elizabeth shrugged her shoulders in silent admission to the woman's astuteness. She would have given her even less information, would certainly have reported her to Maggie, and under the circumstances, perhaps even to the police.

"Suppose," Elizabeth put forward warily, "suppose you did find this statue. What would you do then?"

"Return it to Bangkok on the first flight leaving Pattani."

"But what if you were challenged?"

Elizabeth's questions did not surprise Su-Ling; she would have done the same thing were she confronted with someone claiming to be an agent for Bangkok authorities, and her replies were quiet, straightforward, and to the point. "There is another agent living here in the city who is helping me."

"The man in the truck."

Su-Ling ignored the interruption. "We are prepared to defend ourselves and the statue."

"Against the Moslem faction?"

"Yes." Su-Ling's voice was soft but deadly, and Elizabeth didn't doubt for a moment that this woman would take every protective measure necessary. It was quite likely that she had a gun in her possession and, with that dispassionate Asian nature, wouldn't hesitate to use it.

"Your friends have probably been kidnapped," the woman predicted without feeling. "It would be better for everyone if you would tell me where the statue is."

The weight of a probable kidnapping settled down on Elizabeth's mind, causing her to react more sharply than she had intended. "How would that help them!" she snapped. "Your having possession of the statue wouldn't get anyone's release, because I don't believe you would give it up for the lives of two foreigners." Thoroughly agitated now, Elizabeth was in no mood to humor anyone; spitefully, she wanted Su-Ling to experience the same misery she felt, and so she denied any knowledge of the statue.

"I don't know what this statue looks like. I don't know where it is. And I wouldn't tell you if I did."

Su-Ling's eyes narrowed a fraction, and then she stood up, smoothing the wrinkles out of her black skirt. "Perhaps by morning you will change your mind, when you have wondered long enough about your friends. It will be dark soon. The men working on the roof will go home, in pedicabs." Moving toward the hallway, she stopped beside Elizabeth's chair. "I will wait in my room for the truck to return. Our agent will have news. Then I will speak to you again." And with those significant words hovering in the air, she turned and left the room.

Alone, Elizabeth sank back against the chair, aware of the tension she felt under this new strain. She lifted her hair from the back of her neck, hoping for a momentary cooling breeze. Before she made any decision or took any action, she was going to sit right where she was and think things through.

First, she knew it wasn't prudent to trust Su-Ling completely. The woman had no identification, no proof to match her words. It was possible that she was an agent for the Thai government and intended to return the statue to its proper place. On the other hand, she could be a Communist agent, sent to find the statue and abscond with it at the first possible opportunity. In southeast Asia such actions were entirely within the area of chance. On second thought, Elizabeth mused, it was more in the area of probability. Whatever the case, Elizabeth knew she must be careful and vigilant in the woman's presence.

All of a sudden she realized that Martin was still asleep and had not heard this revealing conversation. As soon as possible, she must alert him to the afternoon's events. She hoped he would awaken soon. She was so anxious to discuss everything with him! He needed to know about Jonas and Maggie, whatever their position might presently be, for he knew what plans had been made with the Chinese pastor. And he also would know what to do about Su-Ling. Perhaps he was awake now; it was suppertime, and he might be hungry.

Elizabeth stood up, hesitating a moment as she wondered whether to return the keys to Maggie's room. Almost immediately, she decided to keep them, to be sure they didn't fall into unfriendly hands. *If anyone uses that jeep,* Elizabeth thought, *Martin or I will be in charge.*

Creeping silently down the hall, she stopped at Martin's door and looked in. Apparently asleep, he was nevertheless restlessly tossing his head. Concerned about a reaction to medication or infection, she hurried to his bedside and leaned over to feel his forehead. He didn't seem to have a fever, but that was a difficult thing to decide in the tropics, where everyone almost always felt warm.

She sank down on the edge of the bed to watch him for a few minutes, wishing he were awake, wondering what he could do if he were. *What would be the first thing he would want to do?* she wondered. The response came quickly. "Find Maggie and Jonas, and the statue," she whispered.

The statue. What had Maggie said about the statue? Elizabeth mentally reviewed their conversation, trying to put her finger on some clue, some hint about its location.

Just then Martin opened his eyes and looked dazedly about the room, focusing last on her. Gradually a weak grin spread over his face.

"That was some knockout pill," he slurred. "What time is it?"

"Almost six o'clock. How are you feeling?"

He blinked his eyes several times, then pulled a reply from his drugged mind. "Great. I'm floating about six feet off the ground."

"Does your arm hurt?"

He made a face and shook his head. "Only when I move." And he did not want to consider moving; every inch of his body hurt from the beating he had taken.

"Are you hungry?"

He considered this a moment and then replied, "Thirsty."

Elizabeth stood up. "Lie still. I'll get you something."

He reached out the hand of his good arm to stop her. "Where's Jonas? I want to talk to him."

Elizabeth hesitated, reluctant to break the news. "Elizabeth, what's wrong?"

"Jonas went with Maggie," she sighed, sinking back down on the edge of the bed. "A Malay mother came asking for help for her sick child, and Maggie insisted on going."

Martin grinned once more. "She would," he murmured.

"Jonas wouldn't let her go alone," Elizabeth continued. "I think he felt it was a trick."

Martin nodded. "Probably the UMF."

"That's what Su-Ling thinks."

Martin's eyes snapped open. "Explain that!"

Elizabeth reluctantly complied, telling her brother about the conversation she had just had with the Chinese woman. When she was through, she whispered, "Martin, did Maggie tell you where it is?"

"No, not a word."

"I wish we knew." Elizabeth propped an arm on her knee and cupped her chin in her hand. "I have a feeling we're going to need it to rescue Maggie and Jonas." She silently contemplated the problem, then sighed and stood up.

"Well, I'll go get you something to drink." Martin tried to sit up, but she commanded, "Lie still. You'll start bleeding again, and Maggie said that could be dangerous."

Defeated by the drugs and his strength completely sapped, Martin sank back against the pillow and waved his acquiescence.

Elizabeth stepped through the kitchen door to find supper ready. She thanked Maggie's servant girl and then called Su-Ling. "Supper is ready," she announced softly.

Elizabeth set a glass of fruit juice on a tray for Martin. Su-Ling watched her silently for a moment, then filled a plate and sat down at the table. As she transferred a small helping of fried rice to a plate, the mosque drums began beating out their nightly call to worship. Elizabeth gasped, nearly dropping the plate. "That's it," she muttered, a spoonful of rice poised in mid-air. "Just as surely as my name is Elizabeth Thurston, I know where Maggie hid that statue."

"What did you say? Did you speak to me?"

Elizabeth's eyes darted over to the table to find Su-Ling's dark, brooding eyes staring intently at her. "The food's hot," she insisted blandly, wondering just what she had spoken aloud. *How much had Su-Ling actually heard?* Restraining her desire to rush to Martin with the news, Elizabeth took her time preparing the tray. At last she started out of the kitchen.

"I want to assist you and your friends," Su-Ling offered suddenly. "I have connections. You are going to need help to prevent someone being killed. You must trust me."

Elizabeth stood frustrated in the middle of the room, nervously gripping the tray. She desperately needed someone she could truly trust, yet something in Su-Ling's nature provoked concern and hesitation. It was like picking a rose to enjoy its beauty, only to be pricked by a thorn.

Perceiving Elizabeth's hesitation, Su-Ling pressed her advantage. "You know where the statue is," and shook her head

at Elizabeth's denial. "Yes, you do. I could see it on your face.
Is it here in the house? Some place nearby? Tell me. I must
know if I am to help."

"I'll eat after Martin is finished," Elizabeth answered, ignoring the questions. "Please don't wait for me," she added as she
left the kitchen. Once inside Martin's room, she placed the tray
on a low table near the bed and roused him from his lethargy.
Ignoring his sleepy reluctance, she put several pillows behind
his back, cautioning him not to sit up too far.

"What's on your mind?" he asked as he forced himself to
eat a little of the food, awkwardly using his left hand. "You
look quite satisfied."

"Eat," was all she would say, and smiled. "You're too suspicious."

Soon he dropped his head back against the pillows and
closed his eyes. "That's all I want," he muttered, leaving half of
the rice on the plate. "Too much medicine. Don't want food."

Elizabeth eased the pillows from behind his back and
helped him lie down again. As she turned to pick up the tray,
he murmured her name.

"Liz, what do you need to . . ." His voice trailed off into a
whisper, "to tell me?"

Martin pushed every word out of his mouth as though he
was squeezing the last pinch of toothpaste from the tube. In his
present euphoria, he found it exhausting to generate much concern over their difficulties.

Elizabeth watched his face for a moment, debating the wisdom of telling him what she had discovered, or thought she
would soon discover, if Su-Ling hadn't heard her mutterings.
He couldn't go with her in his present condition without endangering his life. Perhaps it would be best to wait. If she told him
just before leaving the house, she could prevent him from doing
anything foolish.

Elizabeth returned the tray to the kitchen and sat alone at the table, absentmindedly eating her supper while trying to decide how to keep Su-Ling out of the picture. She could ask the woman to sit with Martin, saying she needed to sleep, but she didn't think that would work. Su-Ling might hear her leave the house and try to follow, and this was one thing Elizabeth planned to do alone.

It might be nice, Elizabeth thought, wrinkling her nose, *if I could slip some of Martin's medication into Su-Ling's tea. That would put her to sleep as fast as blowing out a kerosene lamp; she wouldn't hear anything for awhile!* But it would be hard to pull that trick over on Su-Ling. *I'll just have to wait until I'm sure she's asleep tonight,* Elizabeth decided. *As long as I get away before she discovers I'm missing, she won't know where to look. I'll just have to decide later where to hide the statue so that no one knows I've got it.*

The noise of the workers' truck interrupted her thoughts, and she jumped up and ran to the window. Su-Ling, who had heard it also, was out the front door standing beside the ancient vehicle before the motor cut off. For a long time, she spoke in low tones with the driver, who did not leave his seat. Finally, the motor turned over and the truck backed out of the drive, sputtering in protest as it retreated toward town.

Elizabeth met Su-Ling in the front room. "Well, what did he say?"

Su-Ling's face was difficult to see in the shadows of early evening, but her voice was level and exacting. "He followed. They are prisoners. By the Moslems."

"Did he talk with anyone?"

"No. But a messenger will come tonight, tomorrow, sometime." Su-Ling shrugged her shoulders. "With instructions for you."

"And in the meantime, what will happen to my friends?" Elizabeth tried to keep her voice as level and emotionless as Su-Ling's, but she wanted to explode with anger and fear.

Once again Su-Ling shrugged her shoulders carelessly. Then she turned to leave the room.

"What are you going to do?" Elizabeth asked, still angry at the situation, and especially at the lack of information Su-Ling was giving her.

"I will soon go into town," Su-Ling replied. "I have business."

Good, Elizabeth thought as she followed the woman down the hallway. *I also have business.*

Elizabeth was standing at the worktable, lighting a lamp to take into Martin's room, when Su-Ling came into the kitchen.

"You must stay here while I am gone," Su-Ling informed her without preamble. "Do not leave. It would not be wise." Then she turned and left the house.

Elizabeth waited until Su-Ling's pedicab could no longer be seen in the growing darkness, then she went into Maggie's room to look for appropriate clothing for her adventure.

ò.   ò.   ò.

There were others in Pattani that night who were involved in adventures of their own. Two men ducked down behind an airplane parked at the edge of the Pattani airfield. Dressed in khaki shorts and black shirts, they carried heavy duffel bags which they gingerly placed on the ground. They watched the security guard make his final round of the night, hiding from the bright beam of his flashlight as it made a cursory search of the area.

"Put it here," one man whispered, his heavy accent as thick as the growing darkness. "Here. Not so noticeable."

"Good," his compatriot replied. "We'll tape it to the wheel and set the timer."

The foreigner understood more of the Malay language than he could speak, and in halting words he whispered, "This one," pointing to his duffel bag and then to the terminal building. "Put there. Tomorrow, poof! Everything gone." They finished their work beneath the plane and slid through the shadows toward the terminal.

No one used burglar alarms in the south, and earlier in the day the guard dog had been fed poisoned meat. It was a simple matter to pick the lock on a rear wooden door. The two cautiously felt their way into the darkened building.

Five minutes later they crept outside, replaced the lock, and then hid behind some stacked boxes at the far end of the field to wait for a jeep that was to pick them up.

The Malay laughed softly. "Tomorrow will be a noisy day in Pattani."

The foreigner spat on the ground. He had learned one Malay phrase well, and he growled, "Teach the infidels that we mean business!"

> *He also took hostages.*
> The Book of the Kings

Neither man seated in the front of the jeep bothered to look at or speak to the foreigners. Maggie was accustomed to their driving style, but Jonas thought they had only one goal: to terrorize their passengers with as much reckless driving as was conceivable while delivering them to the proper destination in the shortest possible time.

Jamming the accelerator to the floor, taking the corners on two wheels, and racing for the right-of-way was the normal driving style in south Thailand, producing a near-continuous stream of patients at local hospitals.

Jonas glanced over his shoulder at the road behind them. Headlights shining in the distance seemed higher off the ground than those of a jeep, similar to those mounted on the large, cumbersome delivery trucks used in the country. But whether the truck was racing out of town toward a coastal city or was following them, he could only speculate.

Crowded in between Jonas and the Malay woman, Maggie jammed her back up against the seat, her feet against a metal rod. Ignoring the wild driving, she concentrated instead on the route they were taking. If they turned east at the next intersection, their destination would probably be the Golok Village and a sick child, but if they continued straight through town, then she and Jonas were probably hostages.

The Malay woman's frightened expression could indicate worry about a sick child or fright at the reckless jeep careening down the road, or someone who had been coerced into pulling the foreigners into a trap. A moment later Maggie had her answer. "Well, that's it," she said to Jonas as they drove straight through town and then turned northeast. "We aren't paying a medical visit; this woman's village is south, not north."

Jonas nodded. They had already left the outskirts of town when he turned to find, not at all to his surprise, that the Malay in the front seat had pulled out a gun and, with a malicious grin, had pointed it in his direction. There was no question now of their position; escape from armed captors would be much more difficult.

The road they were traveling wasn't as wide or as well paved as the city streets, and the jeep hit each puddle with heartless accuracy, jarring the passengers and seriously challenging the vehicle's stamina. Although Maggie had traveled by herself in this area dozens of times before, never had she felt this kind of isolation born not of solitude, but of danger. Staring at the gun she nearly succumbed to the despair created by the wildness of the night. Then anger licked through her mind. Fear was the weapon used by the enemy to intimidate, and by God's grace she would fight it with every speck of energy she could muster. A promise from the psalms of King David came into her thoughts, and she found strength in its message: "[The LORD] delivered me from my strong enemy" (Psalm 18:17, RSV).

In the growing darkness the palm trees along the roadside swayed wildly in the wind and thrashed out over the jeep like giant blackbirds pouncing on their prey.

Suddenly, a loud cracking sound penetrated the noise of the jeep engine, and before anyone could react, a giant palm split from its base and toppled slowly toward the road. The falling tree was on a collision course with the jeep! All five passengers threw a hand up for protection and grabbed for something to hang onto as locked brakes tossed the jeep first one direction and then the other. The scene played out in slow motion toward an inevitable impact. The tree fell forward over the road, the jeep skidding into its path. Everyone waited for the impact, wondering how hard they would be hit and what injuries they would sustain.

Finally, the tree hit the road just as the jeep stopped, its nose buried in palm leaves.

Maggie stared at the tree, slightly numb from their narrow escape, her heart thudding. She turned to look at Jonas. He took a deep breath in relief while assessing their situation. He was no fool. He didn't wish to give his life playing hero, but in that moment he decided there wasn't going to be a kidnapping without a fight, and he might not find a more favorable moment. Both the Malays were staring spellbound at the tree. He leaned forward to attack the gunman, but just then the driver turned, arresting Jonas's movement. "Everyone out of the jeep. We have to move that tree," he ordered.

"Have you gone mad?" his companion argued. "That tree is too big! We need a dozen men to move it."

"Quiet! We don't have a dozen men, and we can't just sit here! Do as I say, all of you!" The driver jumped out of the jeep. "Get out!" he ordered, and everyone responded instinctively to his harsh directive.

Still mumbling in protest, his friend stood up, and with the gun aimed at the foreigners, swung a leg over the side of the jeep and stepped out. As Maggie followed, Jonas whispered, "Stay close to me and be ready to run."

They waited outside the headlight beams while the two Malays assessed the situation, one man protesting that it couldn't be done, the other barking at him to shut up. Finally the driver made a decision. "We can't move the tree, but we can clear away enough of the palm leaves to make a path for the jeep. Here, start breaking them off."

It was the opportunity Jonas wanted. He hung back as the Malay woman followed the driver around to the other side of the tree. All three kidnappers were bent over, snapping off fronds and throwing them to the side of the road.

Jonas moved up beside the gunman, reaching forward as though he were preparing to help. Then his fist shot out at the man's head, and he grabbed for the gun.

The driver took two leaps through the mass of palm leaves to come to his countryman's rescue, but Maggie was waiting with the blunt end of a frond. When he cleared the last part of the tree, she swung it as hard as she could, hitting him squarely in the head.

"Allah!" he yelled, grabbing his face, and Maggie attacked again, shoving him hard with both hands. He fell back into the tree, his head hitting the ground with a sharp crack, and then he was still. Maggie dismissed him from her mind and turned anxiously toward the two men locked in battle.

Jonas had the Malay by the wrist, and as they wrestled for possession of the gun, it pointed skyward like a lethal Roman candle at a Fourth of July fireworks display, changing directions at every punch and counterpunch. Jonas doubled his fist and came in with a blow to the chin, but the Malay's free arm blocked it with a short chop at Jonas's throat, followed by a solid one to the stomach.

The enormous shadows, distorted from the closeness of the jeep lights, stretched out over the road and mixed in with the palm fronds. It was difficult for Maggie to separate the two figures. Somewhere in the darkness was the threatening presence of the driver, and the woman must have taken to her heels once she saw the fight begin. Maggie could see only two people on the road, and they were locked in deadly battle, neither one able to overcome the other.

The Malay lashed out with a well-aimed foot in typical Thai boxing style. Too close to be effective, it nevertheless grazed Jonas's leg, throwing him off guard for a second. A fist followed in the mouth, and Jonas grunted in pain.

Sensing the Malay relax slightly in anticipated victory, Jonas brought his fist up with a smashing blow into the stomach, grabbed a hand, and with one flip had the man lying flat on his back on the ground.

Jonas held the gun and backed away quickly, his eyes darting from his opponent to the fallen tree, his hand reaching out for Maggie's. "Stand up," he gasped, his breath ragged with pain, and he motioned for his opponent to move into the light. Out of the corner of his eye he saw the driver, a knife gleaming in his hand, struggle across the palm fronds, stopping short when he saw his partner staggering to his feet.

"Drop the knife," Jonas ordered, stepping to the right to keep both men in gun range. "Hand over the keys." At the man's hesitation, Jonas raised the gun and barked, "Now!" Carefully, the driver put a hand into his shirt pocket and pulled out the keys to the jeep, holding them straight out in the gleaming headlights.

"Maggie, get them," Jonas said quietly, issuing orders as she moved cautiously forward. "Stay to the side, out of my line of vision. There, don't go any closer."

He took a deep breath as she reached his side, keys in hand. Perhaps they had a chance after all. He kept the kidnappers at bay with the gun while Maggie got into the jeep.

"Get it started, Maggie," he said, and then, suddenly aware that someone was missing, asked, "Where's the woman?"

"Here," replied a timid voice in the shadows near the jeep.

There was nothing threatening in the woman's reply; she had no plans to touch Maggie, let alone hurt her, but it jerked Jonas off-balance, and in that split second, the Moslem charged.

Lashing out with one foot, he knocked the gun from Jonas's hand. The other foot followed with a swift kick to the side of the head. The blow wasn't strong enough to knock Jonas out, but it threw him against the jeep and sent his world spinning wildly for a few minutes. He heard Maggie cry out and saw a hand reach out and grab her by the hair.

"Get back into the jeep," the man ordered, holding the gun at Maggie's temple, "or I'll use this. Get in," he ordered at Jonas's hesitation.

Reluctantly, Jonas rolled his aching body around, grabbed on to the side of the jeep, and drunkenly pulled himself into the back seat. He slumped down, touched the side of his head gingerly, and watched his assailant push Maggie towards the jeep.

"Let her go," Jonas mumbled, his head pounding, and his tongue thick. "She can't hurt you."

But the man took delight in revenge, and he twisted Maggie's head around until she moaned, all the while grinning at Jonas with malicious amusement. Finally, he shoved her back up against the jeep, leaving her gasping for breath as she struggled back in and sank down beside Jonas. The woman followed, and in a moment the driver put the keys into the ignition and wrenched around in his seat to confront his prisoners.

"You try that again," he hissed, "and I'll let him use that gun! By Allah's name I swear it! Do you understand me, foreigner?"

Jonas nodded. "I understand."

With terse instructions to his partner to keep the gun trained on their hostages, the driver turned and put the jeep into gear. They started around the tree, backing up several times to keep from sliding into a ditch full of water on one side and getting stuck in the muddy road and palm fronds on the other.

Once they were safely through, he drove another five minutes, then twisted the wheel sharply to the right, throwing everyone off balance. The jeep bounced onto a dirt road, slid sideways through the mud into a tire rut about two feet deep, and came to a jolting stop. The Malay swore his wrath at Allah once more, turned off the motor, and cut the lights.

Flickering timidly through the rubber trees ahead were the kerosene lamps of a small village that was too far away to give any light, and at the driver's command, Maggie and Jonas crawled out of the jeep and stumbled blindly over the ruts to the side of the road. There, hidden in the darkness at the bottom of a steep embankment, identified only by an unmistakable rushing sound, was a river, swollen and swift from the rains.

Still guarding their hostages, the two Malays argued about the jeep, one wanting to hide it from view, the other insisting they didn't have time nor the means to pull it from the mud.

Jonas still held Maggie's hand, and they tried to get their balance in the darkness. "Do you know where we are?" he whispered.

"Yes, and it's not friendly territory. Jonas, you've been watching the road. Is someone following us?"

"Perhaps," he murmured, not wanting to raise her hopes needlessly. "But they'll come to a dead-end here. All they'll find is an empty jeep stuck in the mud."

The driver finally won the argument. Ordering his companion down to the river, he turned to the woman and, with a few sharp words, ordered her to go home.

"This must be her village," Maggie whispered when the woman scurried off into the darkness without a word of complaint.

After watching the woman disappear through the trees, the driver gave Jonas a shove. "Go," he ordered, "and stop talking!"

With only the small beam of the man's flashlight to follow, Jonas and Maggie held on to each other and slid rapidly down the wet, muddy embankment to the river. In a moment they were seated in a small dugout, the Malays using their oars to guide the boat through the dangerously swift water.

"Sit as low as you can," Jonas told Maggie, "and hang on to me." Straining through the darkness, Jonas was the first to sight the lights of a second village along the river. He squeezed Maggie's hand in warning, and as she looked up the boat pulled up to a small dock.

"Get out," the driver demanded, unconcerned about the two foreigners' struggle as they stepped out onto the rotting planks. The boardwalk led up the shore and past a square-shaped, leaf-covered platform that sheltered waiting passengers from the tropic sun or rain. A string of electric lights hung over the scene, illuminating the beach crowded with dark-skinned men and curious children who silently stepped back to make a path for the strangers.

Jonas's steadying hand helped Maggie over the debris of rotting palm leaves and fallen trees which the local people never bothered to remove, and in a moment they stood facing the central part of the village.

The usual number of unpainted, grim-looking shops squatted around the dirt square like stacks of old, useless lumber. Pressurized gas lamps hanging from the door posts of several shops hissed softly in the silence. Stilted huts hovered in the background, sheltering the women who had closed their shutters at the first hint of dusk for protection against the evil spirits that haunted the nights.

Straight ahead in the center of the square was another palm-covered platform, larger than the one by the river. This was the place where the men gathered to gossip in the heat of the day and to conduct business whenever it couldn't be avoided.

As they neared the platform, Maggie could see several men seated there; an older man wearing a haji hat seemed to be the leader. Even as they approached, he was being served a plate of food, and he was issuing orders in a quiet, cold voice.

The young man next to him played continually with a small dagger, and his eyes sparkled in the light of the kerosene lamp. The fanatic look on his face sent a shiver down Maggie's back. A third man leaned against a platform post. Maggie grew angry when she saw that it was the man who had instigated the riot at the morning market. He looked quite pleased with himself.

Maggie looked at Jonas with great concern in her eyes. This wasn't going to be an easy encounter.

CHAPTER 11

*In the night he steals forth
like a thief.*

The Book of Job

T he rain stopped as quickly as it had begun, and the steaming darkness that followed was suffocating. A lone figure
hiding among the trees shivered against the heavy dampness in
the air. The night was saturated with unseen dangers.

Armed with nothing more than a small flashlight, the figure
crept across the open courtyard surrounding the mosque not far
from Maggie Hathway's home. Dressed in a faded sarong, a
man's black shirt, and a Moslem hat, the intruder tread gingerly
through the darkness in thongs that were small protection
against a tropical night's dangers. The greatest danger, how-
ever, was the severe consequences of trespassing on Moslem sacred premises.

Pressed against the building, the sarong-clad figure ignored
the water dripping off the roof. The rain was actually a bless-
ing, since few people ventured out for an evening stroll during
the wet season. The figure poured every ounce of energy into
making a noiseless, unseen approach toward the open porch
that extended out one end of the mosque and faced the street.

At the corner of the building the figure stopped to make
sure there weren't any men using the dry porch area for an

evening's visit. There would be no worshipers at night, but Malays were a sociable, highly curious people.

Mounting the porch steps, the dark form knelt down to examine the large wooden box that encased the lower part of the drum, prying open a loose board near the floor. This had to be the hiding place. After all of the whispered clues, this just had to be it!

And there it was, the object of the night's search—small, wrapped in a faded sarong, and stuck up in the far corner—exposed now to the weak light that came from a partially concealed flashlight. Steady hands worked swiftly, pulling out the bundle, checking the contents, and pushing the board back into place.

Suddenly the intruder's hands were stilled. From the road came the unmistakable clopping sounds of the wooden shoes so popular in southeast Asia. Crouched behind the drum, the figure peered up over the porch railing to see the wide beam of a flashlight dancing across the pavement, guiding two men who had apparently cut through the village across the street and were now coming toward the mosque.

It was too late to run to the palm trees for cover, for even in the dark the open courtyard gave no protection. The only thing to do was to remain hidden and hope they walked on past the porch.

Just then, as if in thunderous defiance of the intruder's wishes, the skies opened up to dump sheets of water down on everything in sight, sending the men scurrying for the cover of the porch steps. The intruder cradled the bundle in one arm, absent-mindedly noting its unusual weight, while measuring the distance to the opposite steps and wondering if it were possible to escape unnoticed.

The attempt had to be made. The trespasser crept to the porch railing, hoping to blend in with its dark shadows. If the heavy rain continued for any length of time, the night strollers could very easily decide to spend the rest of the night on the porch. And a thorough soaking was better than discovery.

The men's voices were barely audible as the rain beat down on the shelter. One of them played with the flashlight, and its beam bounced off the rain and over the building itself. By the time the intruder had crawled to the end of the railing and started down the steps, the rain had stopped. The squishing sounds of wet thongs seemed to echo in the open porch.

"What is it?" one of the men called out in Malay, and as the intruder ducked around the end of the building, the flashlight beam played over the steps.

"You dream," the other man laughed. "Let's go."

"But I saw something," the first man insisted. The noise of his wooden shoes clopping across the porch propelled the intruder across the open courtyard and into the momentary safety of the palm trees.

The flashlight beam moved over the porch and courtyard, and then searched further. Just as the light reached the palms, something splashed softly into the flood waters that swirled ankle deep. The intruder dared not move, even with the knowledge that in all likelihood a snake had just dropped from a palm frond.

For several excruciating moments the flashlight played over the area, then it flickered and went out. The owner swore in his own language and thumped the instrument several times in his hand. "It has died," he finally complained.

There was silence—so long that the figure in hiding among the palms grew increasingly anxious, wondering what the men were planning to do.

The darkness was worse now that the flashlight was dead. It was not wise to begin a blind walk through the trees and flood waters of the nearby river, nor to tread on some unseen snake.

But to stand there all night was impossible. Then came the sounds of the wooden shoes clopping back across the porch and the laughter of the two men as they stumbled across the darkened courtyard on the other side of the mosque.

The intruder's furtive walk back to a house a half mile away was no easier. The need to escape notice added to the strain of creeping through the darkness, of stumbling into bushes and stepping in puddles, of thinking that every large shadow was someone in pursuit rather than a palm tree, and of reaching safety with the bundle intact.

After checking to make sure the house wasn't being watched, the figure crept up the back steps, quietly pulled the door open, and ducked inside. Once there, wet thongs came off, and the small flashlight was turned on long enough to prevent any stumbling or bumping into furniture. Passing through the darkened kitchen, the silent form paused at the Thai-style bathing room and flicked the light across its contents.

A waist-high shelf running along one wall held a soap dish, several towels, and a metal basin. There was a mirror over the shelf, and a few clothes hooks decorated the other walls. Just inside the door sat a small wooden bench, and in the opposite corner a big-bellied earthen water jar completed the furnishings.

This is the place, the shivering figure thought. This would do quite well.

A quick trip was made into the kitchen and then back into the bathing area. There was the rustle of plastic, then a small splashing sound, and then — silence.

Finally, a kerosene lamp was lit and set on the shelf. The Moslem hat was removed and laid on the bench. The figure turned, looked into the mirror, and with shaking hands, slowly reached up and pulled out several hair pins to release a mass of curly brown hair.

"Good evening, foreigners." The leader's voice rang out over the clamoring mob that crowded the village square. The crowd waited eagerly to see what judgment would be meted out by Haji Met.

Maggie returned the Haji's greeting in his own language, but said no more. She could be as restrained as he, and if he chose to play the game of silence, she would also. Unflinching, she returned his stare and waited. Jonas's solid presence beside her was a calming influence against the eager excitement pulsating through the crowd. "I know what the condemned must have felt when they stood before the French guillotine," Maggie whispered ruefully. "There's no compassion in their religion, and this mob is calloused against mercy!"

But it was the older Haji enthroned on the platform, not the crowd, who commanded the respect of every man in the square and who now issued the challenges and decrees. He smiled slowly, almost as though reading her mind, then broke the silence. "Welcome to our humble village, Che' Hathway. Are you well?"

She nodded slightly. "I am well."

"Good. Your companion, what is his name?"

She turned to look at Jonas, and still speaking Malay, replied, "This is Che' Adams. He lives in Bangkok."

"Ah, Bangkok," Haji Met responded as though he were impressed. "This," he said, motioning to his right, "is Hasim, son of Haji Met. A lover of weapons."

Hasim's contemptuous attitude toward foreigners was ill-concealed, and his agitation and the tilt of his head spoke volumes of what he would do with them if he were in charge.

"Friendly fellow," Jonas whispered dryly.

The Haji pressed forward in his interrogation. "What is the foreigner's business?"

Maggie translated the question to Jonas, waited for his reply, and then spoke to the Haji. "He is an exporter."

"Why does he come to Pattani?"

Once more she translated the question and then replied, "Just visiting. We are old friends."

"And does he wish to take goods away from us?"

To her right, she saw the man from the Near East push himself away from the post and move nearer. He was listening intently to her conversation with Jonas, and she boldly aimed a question his direction. "Do you not speak Malay, Ahzid?"

The man stiffened and flashed her an angry look. "I do," he growled proudly.

"But not well enough to follow the conversation. Am I right?" Maggie prodded, enjoying the man's momentary discomfort. Somehow it righted their precarious situation just a little.

But the Haji had grown impatient. "Speak Malay, woman," he warned, then repeated his question. "Does your friend take goods from us?"

It was a veiled reference to the reason for the meeting, and Jonas's reply was just as dissembling. "Could you recommend goods native to the south that would please my customers?"

"Perhaps," the old man replied.

Maggie focused intently on the conversation, wary of the Haji's reactions, but she also followed the activities of the men around them. The Haji's son caught Ahzid's eye and nodded, then slowly ambled into a group of men crowded around the platform. He moved through the crowd, whispering to the men as he went, and soon voices raised against the foreigners. At first the mocking words brought laughter from the mob.

"White people are the wrong color."

"You've been bleached by the sun."

But as voice added to voice the crowd's mood changed to threatening, angry shouts.

"We don't need foreigners! Go back to your own country!"

"Our religion is pure. Your religion is black, you teach lies!"

Soon the single voices bubbled up into a loud protest from all around the crowd, stirred up by insinuating whispers of Haji's son.

Haji sat quietly fingering his prayer beads, letting the sea of men ferment, anticipating the fear that would grow in the hearts of the foreigners, but when the first rock hit Jonas on the arm, he took control.

Raising his hand, he shouted, "Enough! We are not children at play! Enough!"

It took him a moment or two to stop the mob, and when it was quiet once more, he launched into a blistering tirade, his words spilling out so quickly that Maggie could follow only the gist of his lecture. When he turned back to his conversation with Maggie and Jonas, he aimed his tightly-controlled anger at them. His words were clipped and sharp.

"I am interested in a particular item that you have, Che' Hathway." A warning hand went up as he continued, "Don't deny it. I could leave you at the mercy of the mob" — he nodded toward the men around them — "but they may tear you apart, and I still would not have the information I want." He paused, a thoughtful look passing over his face, then he spoke again. "White man, do you wish to bargain? Silver for silver?"

After hearing Maggie's translation, Jonas spread his hands out and replied, "I do not have the silver you want."

Haji turned his attention to Maggie. "And you, Che' Hathway? Do you have silver?"

"No," she replied, shaking her head.

"But we will convince you to tell us where it is." The Haji's voice was a cold promise of unpleasantries, and Maggie knew it. "After a night of persuasion, I am sure you will be happy to tell us what we wish to know." He nodded to the men standing near Maggie. "Take them away," he ordered.

Maggie and Jonas were grabbed by the arms and dragged through the crowd, many of the men using the opportunity to strike out at the unprotected foreigners. The first blow came from her left and hit Maggie squarely on the back, knocking her to the ground.

"Stop it!" Jonas roared, trying to wrench free of his captors, but they merely laughed and pulled him forward, leaving Maggie struggling to her feet in the middle of a group of angry men. He tried to turn around to help her, but something that stung like a knotted rope struck him across the back, propelling him past the shops and down a narrow lane that ran between a row of huts.

The captors enjoyed their momentary power, mocking Jonas for his weakness, challenging him to try running away, accusing him of being a coward. Twice he fell over logs in the unlit pathway, only to be hauled to his feet by a jeering guard. Finally, the guards pushed him into a small clearing surrounded by a dozen stilted, thatched-roofed huts. As soon as the guards released their hold, Jonas turned and ran back toward the path.

"Maggie," he called. "Maggie, where . . . uh!"

This time the whip caught him around the legs, and he fell forward, landing with a splash in a mud puddle. Still laughing, the guards pulled him to his feet just as Maggie appeared on the pathway.

"Jonas, I'm all right!" she called out, trying to calm him down before he took a severe thrashing for his defiance. "Your mouth is bleeding."

"It's nothing," he grunted. "Where are we?"

"It's a school," she whispered, recognizing the distinctive silhouette of a Moslem religious school for boys. "The huts are used for classes and housing. They're empty now. The boys are on vacation because of the wet season."

"Up," a guard ordered impatiently, motioning toward the ladder of one hut. His patience gone, he wished he could take all of his frustrations out on the white man. He was tired of being pushed around by the UMF leaders, and he was sick of political speeches and nightly raids on government posts. He wanted a little power for himself.

Maggie went first, followed by Jonas and two of the guards. The room was empty except for a few sarongs lying in one corner. The shutters were closed against the night and the rain, but they did not keep out the mosquitos or a variety of other insects and animals.

The guards checked to be sure the room was secure, then they started down the ladder. "Don't try to escape or call for help," one of them warned. "I would take great pleasure in sinking my knife in your back, foreigner!"

"I'm sorry, Jonas. I got you into this mess." Maggie sank down on the floor and huddled against the wall.

"It's okay. Stop blaming yourself. You did what you thought was best; that's all we can do. The rest we leave in God's hands."

"But you've taken a beating once already tonight, and there's no telling what they plan to do to us."

"I would never have let you come alone," Jonas murmured as he began to inspect their surroundings.

Hobbling over to a window, he tried opening the shutters, but they were locked from the outside. Then he inspected the room. Made of woven bamboo and covered with a tiled roof desperately in need of repairs, the interior of the twelve-foot-square hut was dimly lit by the kerosene lamp hanging outside the doorway. Chinese calendars and Asian movie advertisements covered the walls. One corner was badly rotted, and Jonas knelt down to examine it more closely. If only he could pry the bamboo away from the wooden frame, they might be able to sneak out! A harsh reprimand from a guard outside cut short his plan for escape, and he turned his attention instead to searching for some kind of weapon. "Nothing but a pile of sarongs. Wish I had brought my gun!"

"No!" Maggie whispered. "You aren't the kind of man who would use it on another human being!"

"This time I might have. We've got to get out of here somehow, before the conversation really gets serious. Got any ideas?"

Maggie shook her head and slapped at a mosquito. "No, not unless I can make a deal with Haji Met."

Jonas gave up his search of the room, picked up a couple of sarongs, and tried to drape them over Maggie's shoulders. "Might keep the mosquitoes away." Then he sat down beside her. "Are you hungry? We've missed supper."

"No, I've lost my appetite." Now that they were alone, she noticed Jonas's bedraggled condition — evidence of his struggles over the last two hours. One cheek sported a large bruise, his lip was cut and swollen, his shirt was torn, and he was covered with mud.

"Oh, Jonas, I'm truly sorry. I don't know of anyone else in the world who would be such a faithful friend." Tears forced her to hesitate. After a moment she went on, her voice shaking. "You're the — the only one who would do this. I've always been proud of you, Jonas, but I don't deserve such a friend." Leaning her head on his arm, she let the tears come. "I — I've m-made such a mess of everything!"

Jonas reached over to take her hand. "Maggie," he countered lightly, "there's no one I'd rather be in such a mess with than you."

"Don't be nice to me," she fussed, trying to wipe the tears from her face with her fingers.

"Here." Jonas reached for a sarong. "Terrific room service, useful for a towel or a handkerchief or a blanket. Not necessarily clean, but available."

"Jonas," Maggie sniffed, attempting to think of other things, "tell me about Martin and Elizabeth."

"Martin is an expert pilot and already a good friend. He fits in well; going to make a fine co-worker."

"And brother-in-law?" Maggie asked.

"I hope so!" Jonas affirmed, turning to her in surprise. "It's that obvious?"

"Yes, and I'm pleased."

"I've asked Elizabeth to marry me, Maggie, but she keeps backing away." Jonas sighed in the darkness. "She was badly hurt by an ex-fiancé and is afraid to trust me."

"I'm not surprised. You haven't known her very long. Give her a chance."

"I just hope the Lord will get us through this. I want so much to give her the love she deserves. And, I want her love, Maggie. I've been lonely."

"I'm surprised to hear you admit that, Jonas. I never thought you would."

They fell silent, each thinking of the gravity of their situation and wondering how the night would end.

"Maggie, do you think Martin's going to have trouble with his arm?"

Maggie nodded, her voice full of concern. "If he would be quiet for a few days, it would be all right. But I'm sure he's not going to stay in bed while we're in danger." Maggie lowered her voice, and her words came slowly.

"Jonas, Martin is — well, I'm impressed. I like him very much. He's just so comfortable to be with, and well," she chuckled, "it's not often that my intractable nature seems to click with someone else, but with Martin, it's different."

Jonas smiled down at the head lowered against his arm. "And it's not often a man has you at a loss for words, my friend." Then in a more serious tone he added, "You might not get much rest tonight; you'd better try to sleep a little."

"Jonas, do you think they'll torture us?"

Jonas kept his eyes on the opposite wall. "It's likely," he replied softly. "Maggie, where did you put the statue?"

"Don't ask," she interrupted. "I won't tell you. I'll take the responsibility of knowing where it is. As long as they don't know, they can't harm us. Can they?"

There was no need to give the obvious answer. Jonas simply smiled and repeated, "You'd better try to get some sleep."

Maggie did as he suggested and drifted into a fitful sleep, still battling the mosquitoes and her fears. Suddenly, a voice from outside jolted them wide awake. "Foreigners, come out here!"

Jonas helped Maggie to her feet, and with a pounding heart, she descended the steps of the hut to find a circle of men waiting for them.

A kerosene lamp hung from a hut window. Haji Met stood, arms folded, his face stern and implacable. His son Hasim held a gun in one hand and a rope whip in the other, and in the dark shadows Ahzid hovered like a vulture waiting for his first meal.

"Tie him to that tree," Haji Met instructed.

CHAPTER 12

*O Lord, my refuge in the day
of distress . . .*

The Prophet Jeremiah

Elizabeth looked at her watch. Only thirty minutes had passed since she had set out for the mosque, but it seemed like hours. A sense of urgency set her heart pounding; Su-Ling must not know of her recent venture, and even more crucial, Elizabeth must plan some kind of strategy for the night.

Her mind boiled with questions and problems. What would she do if that renegade Malay returned, brandishing his gun in her face? And how could she prevent Maggie and Jonas from being killed? Suppose Su-Ling were the enemy. Would her return to the house later that night bring them even more peril? And how could Martin help in his condition?

She hurried through the hallway, her nerves raw, her body jerking at each small sound, her senses anticipating danger. In her fear, each doorway held the darkest evil; each creak revealed killer's steps. The globe of the kerosene lamp in her hands rattled, and the flame sputtered. Gritting her teeth, she tried to control the trembling but didn't have the power to slow her walk.

Ducking into Martin's room, she placed the lamp on the desk and grabbed his flashlight; it would be so much safer than carrying that potential fire hazard around! She threw a quick glance toward her brother on the way out of the room and saw to her relief that he was still asleep. She had no time for a lengthy interrogation, and besides, she wasn't even sure she *could* explain her actions.

Back in her own room the full weight of what she was doing settled around her. She had gone to the mosque! Only God's intervention could have kept her from harm, and she whispered a prayer of gratitude for her safety and success. Then, realizing she was still in wet clothes, she hurried out of the room and down the hall.

Nervously reaching into Maggie's closet to snatch the first skirt and blouse she could find, her hand hit the shelf, jiggling a framed picture that stood too close to the edge.

Strange, she thought as she grabbed the picture before it fell to the floor. *Why would Maggie keep it here instead of on the dresser?* She tipped it toward the light and gasped, all of the urgency over her recent situation vanishing. She had no thought other than what was embodied in the photograph she held. It was a snapshot of Maggie and Jonas, and their happy expressions were not reassuring!

Elizabeth had once seen a wedding photo of Jonas and his Asian bride, who had died less than a year after their marriage. Now this. Did he have a string of such photographs up and down the coast of Thailand? He did have a gregarious nature, but this was getting ridiculous!

Gone was any thought of anticipated danger as she studied the picture. Was Maggie's ring a wedding band? And Jonas's indulgent smile was ambiguous at best. The setting was Asian, but there was no hint of the reason for the photo. Why was it half-hidden on the shelf? If there was something special in this relationship, why wasn't it out in plain view? Elizabeth's thoughts went back to the evening before when she had watched Jonas greet Maggie eagerly and lovingly. Her stomach churned as she replayed the scene bit by bit, amplifying the greeting, the hug, the looks that passed between the two.

Jonas's declaration of love and his wish to marry her now seemed a mockery. All of the affirmation he had shown in the past two weeks in Bangkok vanished from her mind. The picture she held proved that there was something stronger between Maggie and Jonas than mere friendship!

Elizabeth replaced the photograph on the closet shelf, but it was stamped on her mind, mocking her as she changed and then hung her wet clothes on the hook in the closet, well out of sight. Unsettled, she wandered into the living room, wondering why she always seemed so gullible with men. Wasn't there anyone she could trust? Were they all alike?

Angrily, she indulged in a silent complaint to God. All she wanted was to be loved. She didn't want to play games, to pretend what she did not feel, to manipulate another person's emotions or actions for her own satisfaction. She wanted honesty and affirmation and a sense of dignity that comes from true love.

All the bitterness of her recent fiancé's rejection boiled up in her mind. He had used her, had mocked her hunger for the spiritual and aesthetic, had sought her out when he needed her comfort but then insisted that she stand on her own two feet when she needed encouragement, and at times had treated her more like a servant than a friend. Then he had given her an ultimatum: if she insisted on returning to Thailand, their engagement was off. "They're all alike," she muttered, and then stopped.

This wasn't right. She couldn't allow bitterness to control her again. That crippling emotion had been settled with the Lord the night she and Martin were held prisoners in the old Bangkok temple. As the battered structure had tottered and slid slowly into the rising river, she had relinquished those angry feelings and been given a peace she hadn't had in years.

Did she want all that upheaval back again? Did she really want to be burdened with hatred and locked into such destructive emotions?

Was there a lesson in all this? Did she need to learn that the struggles she thought were settled and behind her would reappear to test her resolutions? She didn't know, but of one thing she was certain: she had to learn to refuse her negative thoughts and not allow old habits of bitterness and mistrust to dominate her life.

Sighing, she pushed her questions aside in favor of more urgent decisions. No matter how fragile her emotions, no matter how important Jonas was to her — all that had to be ignored. Maggie and Jonas's lives were endangered, and she had to help them.

A quick survey from behind the curtained window failed to reveal anyone posted outside, and the jeep still sat in the driveway. Turning away, Elizabeth paced across the room. She would have to check the gasoline. She stopped, surprised. Why had that come to her mind? Was it a warning that this second night in the south would be a busy one?

She turned abruptly and re-entered Martin's room. Jonas had a gun, and she meant to find it. Kneeling, she pulled his suitcase into the light, unfastened the locks, and lifted the lid. She felt like a thief rummaging around in his personal belongings, but she grimaced and continued her search, muttering softly, "Men! Why should I care if he doesn't like me pilfering his gun?"

She was far from proficient with such weapons, but the gun was going to become her property for the night, or until Maggie and Jonas were safe.

"What are you doing?" Martin murmured, pulling himself up in bed. He looked slightly more rested, the heavy lines on his face somewhat more relaxed. But his slow, deliberate movements indulged an aching body.

"Gun," Elizabeth mumbled, still bending over the suitcase. "What? I didn't hear you."

Elizabeth snapped the locks shut, pushed the suitcase back into the closet, and stood up, the gun at her side.

"I found Jonas's gun," she whispered, sinking down onto the bed beside him. "I've got a strange feeling about tonight, and I want it with me."

"Liz," Martin protested, a shaft of pain running in a scowl over his face as he sat forward quickly. "Liz, you don't know how to use that thing. Have you ever in your life shot a gun?"

"Once." Her voice was defiant, her hand out of his reach. "Martin, I don't know Su-Ling's intentions, I don't know when we'll be overrun with gun-happy Malays, and you certainly aren't in any condition to do much!"

He took in the determination on her face and sighed his resignation. "Is it loaded?" he asked.

"I—I don't know," she shrugged. Chagrined at her lack of expertise, she stared at the black object in her hand.

"Here, let me see."

Elizabeth studied him a minute. "I want it back." Her voice was full of a stubborn resolve. Martin nodded wearily and held out his hand, and she let him check the gun, then hid it in her skirt pocket. "No one will know it's there," she murmured with a smile that was meant to encourage her brother.

Martin shook his head. "You've changed, and I don't know if it's better or worse. Liz, a little knowledge is dangerous. If you start waving that thing around, you may get us killed before you learn how to pull the trigger, and—"

A soft knock at the bedroom door interrupted his words. Elizabeth glanced at her brother and stood up, shoving a hand into the skirt pocket. Her fingers curled around the gun, and she waited.

"I have returned," announced Su-Ling quietly. "May I come in?"

Martin nodded to Elizabeth, and she called, "Yes, come in." She wondered how long Su-Ling had been at the door. *Had she heard their conversation?*

The Chinese woman entered the room gracefully, her olive skin glowing in the lamplight. At first sight, Elizabeth was struck once more with the woman's beauty and dignity, yet more than ever she sensed an enigmatic toughness, a relentless spirit, a discipline. But was it a discipline that could be trusted? Elizabeth wished she knew.

"Are you alone?" Elizabeth queried.

"No, my associate is here."

"Tell him to come in," Elizabeth ordered, startled at her own authority and amazed when Su-Ling responded with a nod and left the room.

Martin swung his legs over the edge of the bed, felt the room tip into a quick spin, and hurriedly leaned back against the bedpost. "What are you doing!" he hissed.

Elizabeth, ignoring his question, pulled a chair against the wall next to the bed and sat down. It put her in a good position: close to Martin and far enough away from any surprises that might come from the hallway.

The man who entered the room was the same one who had worked on the roof. Studying him now, Elizabeth could see that he was in his mid-twenties. He had the same toughness as Su-Ling, but his face was more arrogant, and he swaggered when he walked.

"Who are you?" Elizabeth asked, unconsciously taking the initiative.

"Chen," he replied, his eyebrows raised mockingly.

"Why are you here?" She knew the answer even as she asked the question, but her face remained expressionless.

In the ensuing silence she saw the two Asians exchange looks. "Why are you here?" she persisted.

Su-Ling responded. "I want the statue."

Elizabeth silently thanked the Lord for the earlier caution she had felt. She could stare into that inscrutable face without flinching or betraying anything.

"It seems a lot of people want it."

"But you have it," Su-Ling retorted. "I know you brought it back to the house. Chen saw you return. It's here somewhere."

Martin shot straight up at this announcement, groaning softly at the pain. He searched his sister's face but for once in his life he couldn't tell what she was thinking. Fully aware that she was no match for the present company, he prayed for the Lord's overruling hand on any bumbling but well-meaning attempts Elizabeth was about to make. Now he wished he had kept the gun; at least he knew how to use it.

"I have told you before," Su-Ling said, her eyes fixed on Elizabeth, her manner solicitous and patient, "I was sent here from Bangkok to find the statue. The government is anxious for its safety and will pay for its return. And I want to help you. If you keep it, you will be in serious trouble. You surely cannot think you are free from the Moslems. They have kidnapped your friends. Chen saw them; he knows where they are being held. If you try to use the statue to save them, you will only end up being destroyed. You cannot do anything. It will be better for everyone if you turn it over to me now."

As she spoke, an impression began to form in Elizabeth's mind, and shock vibrated up her spine as she sanctioned the idea. Weighing the matter was academic, and she acted without any hesitation. As soon as Su-Ling finished talking, she spoke. "You two are going to take me to the village to get their release."

Had she not been so serious, so sure of her intentions, she would have laughed aloud. Visibly startled, Su-Ling was jerked out of her benign overtures, and she stared at Elizabeth in unbelief, and Martin gasped softly in astonishment. Only Chen registered no surprise. His attitude was no different than if he had been offered tea; he folded his arms across his chest and turned to look at his compatriot, waiting for her to take the initiative.

"What did you say?" Su-Ling asked lamely.

"You two are going to take me to the place where my friends are being held and help me free them. And then, if I can, I will see that you get the statue."

"And how," Su-Ling responded, "do you plan to get them free? We are only three people—"

"Four," Martin interjected, cutting off Elizabeth's protest with a stern look. "You'll not go without me."

Su-Ling continued as though he had not spoken. "We are— what is the expression you use . . . ?"

"Outnumbered!" Martin replied. "She's right, Liz. Be reasonable."

"Why do you think we will help you?" Chen asked, looking more amused than concerned.

"This." Elizabeth pulled the gun from her pocket and with both hands aimed it at the two Asians. "I'm not an expert, but I'm standing close enough not to miss. And I'll shoot at the first sign of resistance. I mean what I'm saying! Now then, Chen, put your hand into your pocket, very slowly, and pull out that gun and put it on the bed."

Chen complied, and Elizabeth instructed Martin to pick it up. After ordering Chen to give up a wicked-looking knife, she checked Su-Ling for weapons as well.

"What are you planning?" Su-Ling demanded, her voice full of anger at this turn of events.

"That depends on what happens when we get to the village. But be assured that I'll trade your lives if necessary."

"But," Su-Ling protested, her voice rising angrily, "I've told you that we are on your side."

"And I have no proof," Elizabeth interjected, "of who you are or what side you're on. I want my friends released, and I'll

do just about anything to see it done — tonight! Do you understand?!"

"You aren't the kind of person to use that gun," Su-Ling
challenged. "We could walk right out of here, and you wouldn't
harm us. What makes you think we will do as you say?"

"Because I'm the only person who knows where the statue
is," Elizabeth answered. "You'll never find it without my help."

When Martin struggled to his feet, she protested. "You
can't possibly go with us. Maggie said that if you moved too
much, you might open your wound."

He waved her objections aside, his eyes on the Asians,
Chen's gun in his hand. "If you're going through with this, I'm
part of the deal." He turned to Chen. "Where are they?"

"At a boys' religious school outside a Moslem village north
of here."

Elizabeth didn't need to look at her brother to feel his
shock at her actions. She was a little shocked herself. Fleet-
ingly, she wondered if she could ever shoot to kill. Was there
some unknown, horrifying monster in every human heart that
would do the most evil deeds if challenged? The need to have
Jonas and Maggie safe again overwhelmed every other thought
or emotion. In a flash of insight, Elizabeth understood why people sometimes took such drastic actions out of fear or love. The
words of the prophet Jeremiah echoed in her mind. Man's heart
was indeed "desperately wicked."

"I must warn you," Chen growled as they left the room,
"the roads are bad. We could get stuck."

Elizabeth, fearful of failure in this rescue attempt, tightened
already tense fingers holding the gun. "For your well-being,
you'd better see that we don't!"

CHAPTER 13

*He who walks wisely will be
delivered.*

The Book of Proverbs

After reassuring herself that Su-Ling could not rummage
under the front seat for a weapon, Elizabeth jumped into
the back of the jeep with Martin and handed the keys to Chen.

The drive out toward the village was uneventful except for
a slight delay while Chen maneuvered the jeep around a large
palm tree that had fallen across the road. The forbidding night
sky hung low, threatening more rain and adding to Elizabeth's
apprehension. In a few minutes, Chen pulled to a stop.

"Keep both hands on the wheel where I can see them," Elizabeth instructed. "Where are we?"

"The village is in there," Chen said, thrusting his chin toward a grove of rubber trees to the right, "but we must leave
the jeep here."

"What about that road we just passed?" Martin mumbled.
He had already moved too much, and the little strength he had
would render a long walk impossible.

"Too muddy. There is already a jeep stuck in the road."

Su-Ling turned with a frown. "That means if we get stuck,
we won't have a jeep for our escape."

Chen shook his head. "We will leave the jeep behind that coffee shop and walk in."

Surrendering the jeep keys to Elizabeth, Chen led the way through the rubber trees, using his flashlight when necessary but making it as difficult as possible for the others to follow. Martin, second in line, tried to keep his gun aimed at Chen while he struggled to remain standing. From her place at the end of the little procession, Elizabeth could see the tremendous effort he was making, and she grew worried. She could hardly keep Su-Ling in full view as they slid along the edge of the dark road; what would she do if Martin couldn't control Chen?

The situation worsened when they left the road to follow a path that wound its way around a cluster of huts. Here they had to do without Chen's light for fear of discovery. Elizabeth made every effort to keep directions in mind; she had to know the way back out to the road. But it seemed as though Chen was leading them in circles, and the only landmark she recognized was an occasional glimpse of the river.

She was so intent on the trail that she failed to see the next obstacle the others had skirted. As she stepped forward she sank ankle deep into thick mud. "Wait," she hissed, attempting to release herself. It was like trying to pull free of glue, and losing her balance, she grabbed wildly for something solid. It was Su-Ling.

"Pull slowly," the Chinese girl whispered, holding onto her arm and ignoring the gun waving erratically in Elizabeth's other hand. "Pull your foot forward, slowly, up out of the mud. Now," she urged, "step here, on this rock. Now the other foot." The moment Elizabeth was free, Su-Ling dropped her arm and turned to follow the men.

For a second, Elizabeth stood staring after her. The Chinese woman had missed a perfect opportunity to grab the gun. Instead, she had helped Elizabeth out of her predicament and then ignored her thanks. Was she, after all, exactly what she claimed to be? Was she really a government agent, and was this rescue effort a stupid decision made by an incompetent foreigner? In this sudden role as jungle adventurer, Elizabeth's confidence wavered.

It doesn't matter, she thought as she plodded down the path. *I don't care who she is. I want Jonas and Maggie free. It may be wrong, but I've got to do something! I just can't sit waiting for two bodies to be dumped in the frontyard. I've got to try to get to them!*

For another five minutes the four clambered through the darkness over the uneven path. Occasionally, they passed a lighted hut, the murmur of voices rising softly over the rain, but no one else was outside.

Suddenly Martin staggered, threw out a hand to steady himself, then pitched forward against Chen.

"Martin!" Elizabeth cried, lunging past Su-Ling. Thrusting the gun into her skirt pocket, she knelt down and tried to pull him up into her arms. "Martin, are you all right? Martin!"

"Liz," he moaned, "you've got to leave me here."

"No, I won't! I can't!"

"Chen," Su-Ling ordered as she knelt down, "turn your flashlight on. Let me see his arm."

"Oh, Martin." The light revealed a large red blotch on the bandaged arm. The wound had broken open, and he was bleeding again.

"I'll find a place for him," Chen whispered. "There is a hut nearby. We'll take him there."

Supported by Chen and Elizabeth, Martin managed the walk to the thatched-roofed, stilted hut while the owners watched disapprovingly.

The old man, clad in a sarong and undershirt, and with a face like crumpled leather, argued long with Chen; his wife stared silently at this unwanted intrusion into her quiet world. Finally the man nodded reluctantly and helped Chen drag Martin up the ladder and into the hut. Martin's groan of pain tore at Elizabeth's mind and heart, and she ignored Su-Ling's presence in the room. Nor was she concerned with the wife, who was complaining under her breath. Her apprehensions centered on her brother, her thoughts far from her two Chinese companions who might try to make their escape.

"We must get him to the hospital."

"No." Martin was stretched out on a straw mat along one wall of the small room. "Elizabeth," he whispered in a shaking voice, "you've come this far. Don't turn back. Make this worthwhile."

"But you could die if you don't get help." Tears of worry and regret coursed down Elizabeth's cheeks, and she wiped them away with the back of her hand.

His voice was ragged with pain. "Go on. No matter what happens, we can trust God. Even if I die here. We're both in God's hands. We belong to Him."

"God!" Su-Ling exploded. "You foreigners are always talking about your God." She turned fierce eyes toward Elizabeth and sneered, "Is this the way your loving God takes care of you? I don't need a God like that. I can manage better without Him."

Misery washed over Elizabeth, and her eyes widened as she stared into that searing anger. Would her stubborn determination result in Martin's death? *Lord,* she pleaded silently, *forgive my wrong. Help us. Save us from death.*

Martin managed a wobbly smile, "Liz, God will deliver His own. He promised."

"I'll . . . " her voice broke, "I—I'll be back for you." She leaned forward and held her face close to his, wanting to give him some of her strength, the little girl in her silently sobbing for a miracle.

But Chen was forcing her away. "We must go before it is too late," he urged, pulling her to her feet.

With fading hope Elizabeth took a long look at her brother and then left him, alone and at the mercy of strangers who cared nothing for his life. Never before in her life had she ever felt like such a betrayer.

On the path again, Elizabeth's heart was torn with grief. Leaving her brother behind, knowing she might never see him alive again, was almost more than she could bear. How could it come to this? What could she do?

And now her position was far more precarious than before. Outnumbered and completely inexperienced, she could only hope to keep up a tough facade and not become a hostage herself. She mustn't let her mask of authority slip. Resolutely, she forced it back into place.

The rain returned, pouring down so hard that they could barely see more than three feet ahead; and their progress slowed. Elizabeth felt that she was drowning in a world of rain that would never stop, and she took a deep breath to dissipate the suffocating knot in her throat that was pushing her toward hysteria. Chen stumbled into a wayside pavilion, motioning the women onto the platform, which provided partial shelter from the rain. The moment they sat down, Su-Ling taunted Elizabeth again.

"Tell me now about your loving God. If He is so strong, why isn't He helping you? Do you need a gong to summon Him? Is He asleep, like my mother's gods?"

Elizabeth wiped the rain from her face and leveled a challenging look at Su-Ling, waiting for the tirade to stop. Finally she spoke. "Why are you so angry?" she asked gently. "You say you don't believe in my God. Then why do you hate Him so much? I've never understood why unbelievers hate a God they say is not real. Su-Ling, I think your heart is desperate to know the peace my God can give you."

Startled, Su-Ling drew back into silence, unwilling to question her own motives. But after a moment she launched a different attack. "Your brother is about to die, and your friends will probably not live until morning. What do you plan to do now, foreigner?"

"I don't know, but I'm trusting my God. He has promised never to leave me. He'll show me what to do."

Laughter sliced into their conversation with the sharpness of a knife, and Chen spoke for the first time since leaving Martin in the hut. "Perhaps your God has spoken to me. I know what to do," he said softly as he snapped on his flashlight and aimed a gun at the two women.

"Where did you get that?" Elizabeth asked, glancing at Su-Ling's face. It wasn't reassuring to see that she too was surprised.

"It was easy to take it from your brother when he fell," Chen bragged. "And you," he pointed the gun at Su-Ling, "you did not notice. Such a worthless agent. I shall be sure to report that to our superiors."

"What do you think you are going to do?" Su-Ling mocked, her words thick with accent.

His soft reply could barely be heard over the noise of the rain, but it sent a chill down Elizabeth's back. "I am going to kill both of you."

"But you need me," Su-Ling protested.

"No, I don't. The statue is in the mission house." He glanced at Elizabeth. "I can find it without your help. I don't need either of you any more."

"You first." He turned and aimed the gun at Elizabeth's forehead, his black eyes squinting against the rain and darkness.

"You will die, too," Su-Ling said, so confidently that Chen lowered the gun slightly to confront this new challenge.

"No, I am going to get rich."

"Do you not think," Su-Ling went on, "that our leaders have planned for this? How long has it been since you've heard from your family?"

"They are visiting relatives in Chongmai," he retorted, but
the tone of his voice held a slight suspicion.

"No, they are being detained until I return."

"How do you know this?"

"I ordered it," came the curt reply.

"I don't believe you."

"You were sent to the south because you know no one
here; you are far from your friends and family. There is no one
here who will help you."

Chen's look of anger changed to disbelief as Su-Ling reminded him of his vulnerable position, giving him the names of
his wife and children and where they were. An unreadable expression come over his face. He glanced at Elizabeth and then
back at Su-Ling, his swaggering attitude gone. His eyes narrowed, and he turned the gun on Su-Ling. *If I live to sketch a
thousand faces, I will never forget his look of hatred,* Elizabeth
thought. She drew in a sharp breath; he had decided to kill
them after all.

Suddenly, laughter from the far end of the path caught
Chen off guard. He turned is head sharply toward the sound,
and Su-Ling simultaneously brought her hand down hard on his
wrist and grabbed for his weapon. His flashlight fell onto the
ground and went out, and in the darkness he struggled silently
with Su-Ling.

"Stop it, both of you!" Elizabeth ordered in a whisper,
whipping the gun from her pocket and shoving it into the back
of Chen's neck.

"Stop, or I'll shoot!"

The two Asians froze at this sudden turn of events and
stood staring at each other, Su-Ling in triumph, Chen in frustration. Reluctantly, he released his gun, and Su-Ling tucked it
into her waist.

Elizabeth stepped back, not wanting to be discovered by the Malay men who were coming down the pathway, and ordered her captives off the pavilion and into the bushes.

"This gun will be aimed right at you," she warned. "If you make a sound, it will be your last!"

Oh, Lord, she thought in horror as she dropped down behind the bushes, *what have I become! How can one of Your children threaten someone's life! Don't let it come to that. Please don't let it come to that!*

Silently, they waited. A dozen men filed past their hiding place, their conversation about the foreign hostages and their laughter drowning any other sounds along the path. In a moment they were gone.

"Were they searching for us?" Elizabeth asked.

"Doesn't matter," Chen muttered. "We must get away from here before one of them comes back to check." He threw a curious look at Elizabeth. "Unless your God has a better idea."

Elizabeth ignored Su-Ling's mocking laugh and agreed that they needed to push ahead. She thought one of the men had just left the group ahead and turned off into the trees. Had he seen them hiding among the bushes? Was he doubling back to catch them off guard?

"Let's get to that school," she ordered, waving her gun toward the path.

CHAPTER 14

Save me from all those who pursue me.

The Psalmist

I t was a scene from a horror movie, complete with dark shadows impregnated with evil and the threat of death. Elizabeth hated such movies, but had she watched a thousand, she would not have been prepared for the trauma she felt. She was out of her element, away from the comfort of the familiar, thrown into a strange world that little understood the niceties of so-called civilization.

But her fear quickly boiled up into the hottest anger she had ever experienced; she didn't doubt for a moment but that she would willingly use her gun to gain freedom for Jonas and Maggie.

Chen guided them swiftly to the school — so swiftly in fact, that Elizabeth accused him of leading them in circles earlier in the evening so that Martin might be eliminated.

"You deliberately kept us from. . . ."

An anguished cry that exploded through the quiet night cut off her whispered accusation.

"No! Stop that!"

"That's Maggie," Elizabeth whispered, peering through the bushes that hugged the river's edge where they stood hidden from view. "And Jonas!"

The kerosene lamp threw a dull gleam over the group of men who ringed a palm tree in the center of the schoolyard. About eight Malays stood in a semicircle, their attention riveted on the man tied to the palm tree, the back of his shirt torn open. It was Jonas!

A shadowed arm raised and flipped a whip back over a man's head, cutting across Jonas's back with the sound of a stinging wet towel. But this was no towel fight between siblings. Knots on the whip dug deep into the flesh. Jonas moaned; his body stiffened and then slumped, dragging his face down over the rough bark.

"Stop it!" Maggie cried out again in angry protest. "Haji Met, I *demand* you stop this immediately!" She turned toward the Moslem leader and, true to her nature, charged forward to face him, unafraid of what punishment she might receive. She wasn't even aware that two guards grabbed her arms and threw her to the ground at the Haji's feet. She kept right on with her demands until a harsh, ringing response came from the Malay leader. In the quietness that followed it wasn't difficult to hear his soft demand.

"Tell us what we want to know, foreign woman, and we will let you both go free. Surely you know, don't you, that we do not wish to harm anyone. We merely want the statue."

Jonas groaned, "Don't tell them, Maggie!"

She struggled to her feet, undaunted, and stood with her hands on her hips staring back at the Malay. "Give us our freedom; *then* we'll talk about that statue! Not before!"

That brought a nod from the Haji, and the whip came down again, this time with greater force.

The crack of the whip and the sight of Jonas's bleeding back brought Elizabeth out of a numbing paralysis. Turning to-

ward Chen, she ordered, "Get around to the other side of the village and do whatever you must to get their attention. Burn
down a building, rip the place apart, make it sound like the
army has moved in. I don't care what you do! Just do it!"

The Chinese stared at her in surprise. He hadn't expected
this kind of spirit from a foreigner. "How am I supposed to do
that?" he growled.

"That's your problem," Elizabeth responded, leveling her
gun at him. "You were so smart on the trail, deciding you
didn't need us any more. Well, I don't need you here. Now
move!"

He took a prudent step backward, still hesitating. Then he
whispered, "I'll shake the whole village, believe me, but I need
a gun."

Elizabeth glanced at Su-Ling. She didn't trust either her or
Chen. Perhaps it would be better if that gun were on the opposite side of the village. A few shots in the air would stir things
up and just might give them the edge they needed to pull this
thing off.

"Don't do it," Su-Ling warned. "He'll use it on us. He'll
kill us!"

Elizabeth stared at Chen, a hardness clamping down over
her mind like a steel door. "No, he won't. I have my God's protection. Chen, you can take the gun, but listen to me. If I so
much as catch a glimpse of you, I'll shoot and ask questions
later. Do you understand me?"

The man nodded curtly and held out his hand.

"Put your hands in the air and turn around," she ordered.

He frowned but obeyed, slowly turning his back on the
women, wondering if she had decided to shoot him on the spot.

"Su-Ling, put your gun in his belt."

Reluctantly, the woman complied, shoving the gun down
under Chen's belt in the middle of his back.

"Now, *move*," Elizabeth ordered coldly. "And don't reach for that gun until you're well away from here."

With an undefinable grin Chen disappeared into the bushes that surrounded the west side of the schoolyard. Elizabeth backed up against a tree for protection and put Su-Ling to work while they waited for the diversion Chen had bragged about.

"The dugouts are pulled up on shore. Su-Ling, get down there and push all of them out into the river. Save that one nearest us."

Su-Ling's look challenged her, but she nevertheless crept silently down to the river's edge to shove the boats out into the river current.

While she watched Su-Ling, Elizabeth listened to the discussion between the hostages and the Malays, wincing as the whip sizzled through the air toward its target again.

Suddenly, two shots rang out into the night, followed by the uproar of voices and pounding feet. It sounded like complete pandemonium — like a retreating army crashing through the forest. The Malays in the schoolyard turned and ran toward the village, leaving the Haji, who stood cursing at his fleeing compatriots, and Hasim, who still held the whip.

Elizabeth pushed Su-Ling through the bushes, and they burst out into the yard. "Get your hands up," she ordered, pointing the gun at the two men. "Up," she repeated emphatically.

Hasim dropped the whip, and his hands shot up into the air; Haji Met refused to move.

Angrily, she lowered the gun and fired at the ground at the Haji's feet. The shot, barely audible over the din created by Chen's actions, nevertheless brought about the effect she wanted. The Haji slowly raised his hands into the air.

"Maggie, get that knife at the Haji's belt. Cut Jonas loose. Quick. We don't have much time."

Her words penetrated the shock that had enveloped Maggie. She was not hallucinating; Elizabeth really was standing there with a gun!

Elizabeth ordered the two men up into one of the huts and instructed Su-Ling to pull the ladder away from the door. "If you so much as stick your head out that door, I'll shoot," Elizabeth warned, and then felt Jonas's arm go around her waist and his forehead lean against the top of her head.

"You little spitfire," he chuckled, his voice ragged with pain, his body swaying slightly. "Where did you get all this spunk?"

"From being around you this last month," she replied, her eyes still on the door across the yard, her relief at feeling his closeness nearly sapping away the anger she needed to carry this thing through.

"Get to the river, all of you," she whispered, and started backing toward the bushes.

A face appeared in the doorway, and just as she had threatened, she fired the gun. She aimed high into the air, but the Moslems weren't taking any chances. There was no more movement in the doorway.

No one challenged her leadership for the moment. Maggie and Su-Ling ran toward the river and silently got into the boat. Jonas guided Elizabeth. She was so intent on making sure the two men did not follow that she refused to turn around until her feet hit the water's edge and she heard Jonas tell her to get into the boat. The moment she sat down, Jonas gave the boat a hard shove, barely jumping in himself before it hit the swift current of the flooding river.

Maggie had dipped an oar into the current to try to guide the boat, and Su-Ling was crouched down just behind her. But suddenly Elizabeth couldn't move. Every ounce of her strength drained out of her body as if someone had pulled the plug in a bathtub.

Mechanically, she laid the gun beside her feet, folded her hands in her lap, and sat staring at Jonas, hardly daring to believe they had been successful. Tears of relief, of delayed reaction, of gratitude, streamed down her face, and she couldn't even wipe them away.

Jonas reached forward, cupped her face with both hands, and gave her a swift, fierce kiss. He felt the tears washing down over his hands and whispered as he reached for an oar, "Don't cry, my love, we're doing fine, just fine."

Quietly, so as not to be heard by anyone on shore, Su-Ling filled them in on what they could expect. "The jeep is at the main road, behind a shop right near the river. If we can get to it, we'll be free."

Silently, Maggie and Jonas steered, trying to use the speeding current to their advantage. Su-Ling and Elizabeth, knowing they must not be discovered, said nothing.

As they approached the main road, Jonas whispered, "Hard, Maggie, toward shore. We won't have a second shot at this."

Elizabeth could feel the oars jab down into the water as the boat veered slightly to the right, challenging the current, so strong from the rains that it was almost impossible to break its hold.

"Pull," Jonas whispered each time the oars sank into the water. Maggie grunted with every stroke, using all the strength she could muster.

Elizabeth felt her body straining with each attempt, willing the boat toward dry land, demanding that the river let them go free.

They shot toward the shore. "We're going to make it," Su-Ling whispered triumphantly. Then they hit something in the water, perhaps a log or part of a broken pier. The boat spun around, tipped dangerously for a second, righted itself, and was jerked back into the main current. Maggie's oar flipped from her hand in the spin, hit the water with a splash, and disappeared.

They shot right past the main road, the narrow bridge fading from view in a matter of seconds. But Jonas refused to give up. He tried to steer toward the shore, but it was a feeble attempt with just one oar. Their opportunity to get to the jeep gone, they would continue down the river toward some unknown destination — perhaps even further into Moslem territory.

Suddenly Jonas cried out, "Hang on!"

The boat shot through the current at breakneck speed, hit something solid, and came to a jolting stop. Maggie fell forward, slamming into the side of the boat so hard she was knocked breathless. Su-Ling landed on top of her. Jonas dropped the oar, stiffened his legs and grabbed for Elizabeth. On impact they slid down into the bottom of the boat.

"We hit a bend in the river and ran right into shore," Jonas grunted. His back wounds were torn open, but he pulled Elizabeth to her feet.

"A miracle," Maggie said when she finally got her breath. "Thank you, Lord. You do take care of Your children!"

Su-Ling threw her an angry look but said nothing.

They scrambled up the wet, muddy bank of the river and for a few minutes sat on the grass, each one trying to catch their breath and find strength for whatever lay ahead.

"Well, Elizabeth," Jonas murmured, his back throbbing with pain, "you've had a busy two days in south Thailand."

"Two days?! Are you sure it hasn't been two weeks?" she challenged. "My suitcase was stolen, Maggie's house was set on fire, she's been threatened, Martin was beaten up at the marketplace, and you two were taken hostage. That's enough plot for an entire novel!"

"Don't forget your daring rescue," Jonas teased, reaching over and squeezing Elizabeth's hand. He was proud of the way she had taken charge. "What time is it?" she asked.

Jonas checked the luminous dial on his watch. "Two o'clock in the morning. We've got about two hours before sunrise. That should give us plenty of time to get out of here."

Suddenly, Maggie surged to her feet. "Oh, no," she whispered, running down to the river's edge.

"What's the matter?" Jonas asked, gingerly twisting his back to test his injuries; it hurt, but if he could just keep moving, he wouldn't stiffen up.

"You won't believe this," Maggie grimaced as she turned to face the others, "but we're on the wrong side of the river!"

"Are you sure?" Elizabeth jumped up in disbelief.

"Maybe you're turned in your directions, Maggie." Jonas joined the anxious women at the river's edge and tried to take stock of their position.

"We came from that direction," Maggie stated in a tone that would not yield to argument, "and we passed under the bridge and the main road, and the shops were on our right. When the boat flipped around, we made a complete circle. We hit the bend in the river right there. The road is back there!"

Asians believe that touching someone else without permission is extremely humiliating because you may cause the good spirits to leave the body. But Su-Ling was so upset that, totally out of character, she grabbed Maggie's arm and shook her angrily.

"What's the matter? Doesn't your God know directions? If He helped us get to shore, why couldn't He put us on the right side of the river! How stupid! How utterly stupid!"

"Stop it," Jonas growled, pulling Maggie out of Su-Ling's reach. "Standing here screaming about it isn't going to help."

"And what will?" Su-Ling fumed. "Our boat is filling up with water. I do not see another one. Perhaps your God can build us a bridge, or part the water as you say He did for that prophet Moses! Why don't you pray for a miracle?"

"Stop it!" Elizabeth ordered, anger surging through her once more. "Your ranting doesn't help a thing. Of course our God helped us. None of us drowned. We're safe on shore, and we can walk back to the road."

Su-Ling turned on her in a fury. "Do you know how far back the road probably is? We don't have time! A patrol of Malays will be after us in minutes."

"Then I suggest we get busy," Jonas interjected mildly. "We'll start walking back toward the road, on the double."

They stumbled along the edge of the river for about twenty minutes, Jonas holding Elizabeth by the hand as he took the lead. Sometimes they maneuvered their way along the river's edge, sometimes they had to detour around fishing huts, dense brush, and stretches of thick, impassible mud. They didn't seem to be nearer the road or the village or the shops. It was as dark ahead as it was behind them.

Then Jonas stopped. "Motor boat coming," he cautioned.

They ducked into a small tract of coconut trees just as a boat came into view. The motor was cut, and a strong light swept over the opposite shore, then turned toward them. They could hear the men talking, and Maggie whispered an interpretation.

"They've captured a Chinese. He's in the boat, and they're threatening to drowned him if he doesn't help."

"Chen," Su-Ling guessed.

"And if they notice our boat . . ." Elizabeth didn't finish her sentence; she just shivered and drew close to Jonas.

"Let's hope it's full of water by now," Jonas murmured. "They won't think it's ours."

The light swept over the trees and back again before the motor sputtered and turned over. Finally, the boat continued downstream. They had not been discovered. But they didn't have much time.

After stumbling through the darkness for another ten minutes, the fugitives finally found the road, sneaked across the open bridge, and crept past the coffee shop. A few hardy souls were still talking.

When they reached the jeep at last, Maggie suddenly whipped around to face Elizabeth. "Where's Martin?" she demanded.

The question brought Jonas up short. "Is he at home?"

"No," Elizabeth replied, shaking her head. "He's somewhere back there." She nodded back into the jungle toward the village. "He refused to stay behind."

"Dear Lord," Maggie whispered. "He collapsed, didn't he?" Not waiting for an answer, she went on, her voice anxious and demanding. "He refused to let you come out here alone, but his wound started bleeding again, didn't it?"

"Yes," Elizabeth admitted, rubbing her forehead in frustration. "We had to leave him with an older Malay couple, in their hut, somewhere back in there." A wave of her hand indicated the wide expanse they would have to search.

"Then we'll just go find him," Maggie exploded. When she saw Jonas shake his head at that impossible task, she folded her arms resolutely and declared, "We'll find him, Jonas. I'm not going anywhere without him!"

"Oh, yes, you are."

Maggie whirled around at Su-Ling's remark, surprised at the insistence in her voice, ready to argue with her as well. But her words froze on her lips.

Su-Ling stood just a few steps away, facing the other three, holding a gun.

"Elizabeth Thurston, you made a mistake in putting your gun down in the boat. I thank you for making it so easy for me." She waved the weapon toward the jeep. "Get in. We're going back to the city."

Defeated, Elizabeth took the keys from her pocket, handed them to Jonas, and stepped into the jeep beside him.

But Maggie refused to move. "I won't go! Not without Martin!"

"Very well," Su-Ling responded, pushing the gun into the back of Elizabeth's neck. "Move away from the jeep, or I'll shoot her. Get over there against the building."

Startled, Maggie stepped away from the jeep, her eyes never leaving Su-Ling's face, ready to fall to the ground the moment the gun turned in her direction.

"Don't worry, Maggie Hathway," Su-Ling said, "I will not waste a bullet on you. Haji Met's people will take care of you soon enough. You cannot leave this village without being seen by them." She laughed, in a soft mocking tone. "Now go and find your sick friend — if you can."

Jonas Adams threw a frustrated look over his shoulder at Maggie, then following Su-Ling's next instructions, started the motor.

ଈ ଈ ଈ

Martin lay on the floor of the hut, gritting his teeth to keep from passing out and praying aloud for God's protection. Neither of the two attending him understood English; they thought he was incoherent.

The old man watched for awhile, growing more worried by the minute. If the police discovered this man in his house, he would be arrested and probably shot on the spot, no questions asked. Why would anyone believe their story? It sounded ridiculous to the old man, and he *knew* it was true.

Who would believe that all these foreigners had wandered into their hut at that time of night? And that the foreigner had already been injured? No, he would be accused of wounding him. Oh, it would go hard.

"Insha Allah," he muttered, "I don't like this!" In the light of the small lamp made from an old condensed milk can, he watched his wife working with the wound. There was no need to call the local Malay witch doctor; he wouldn't come out on such a bad night, and certainly not for a foreigner. His wife sat on the floor, her ancient legs tucked up pliantly beneath her body, her gnarled hand putting steady pressure against the wound to stop the flow of blood.

The foreigner's eyes fluttered open, and he stared at her, making every effort to concentrate on her presence, on the pain in his arm, on the smell of the kerosene lamp, on anything in order to remain conscious. He turned his head toward the old man. "Do you speak Thai?" he asked, and the old man nodded. "Can you find someone who will take me back to Pattani?"

"No," the old man responded.

"Take me to the main road."

When the old man refused again, Martin persisted, "Show me which way to go." He rolled slowly over on his side, using his elbow for support, and tried to sit up. But the old woman lashed out in a flood of protest and pushed him back down against the mat. Martin couldn't understand a word she said, but he could feel her displeasure.

He stared, fascinated, at her face. Her few remaining teeth were stained with red beetle-nut juice, that narcotic the Malay women so loved. And over those red teeth and barely-moving lips came a stream of unintelligible words that held him completely spellbound.

Finally, she stopped scolding and turned to her husband. Their conversation, in a language he could not understand, added to his growing sense of unreality. Words seemed to spit through the air, the old man disagreeing, the wife making it clear that she could do no more for her foreign patient. In a moment the old man stood up, relayed some bit of terse information to his wife, and left the hut.

After a long stretch of time, perhaps an hour, the old man returned, motioning for Martin to follow. He descended the ladder, leaving the foreigner to make his way the best he could.

Outside on the pathway a *samlo* was waiting. With a nod of his head and a few more unintelligible words, the old man indicated that the Thai-style rickshaw was transportation back to the main road. Martin pulled himself up into the basket seat behind the bicycle, painfully aware that the loss of blood had sapped much of his strength. But no matter how weak, he had to try to get back to the jeep; it made sense to wait there for the others, wherever they were. He could only hope they were safe. He thanked the old man, then sat back with a sigh as the driver started to pedal slowly down the path.

After about three-quarters of a mile they came to the coffee shop at the edge of the main road. It was filled with late-night customers — men enjoying glasses of hot coffee and subdued conversation. The shop lights spilled out over the road, and out of idle curiosity Martin leaned his head to one side to study his driver.

What he saw gave him the shock of his life. The man had a scar running across his cheek. It was the same man who had threatened Maggie's life the night before!

Another surprise followed. Instead of stopping at Martin's command, the driver turned to the right and pedaled on until he pulled up in front of a large wooden house set well back from the road. There were a dozen Malays standing around in the yard.

Martin stepped out of the *samlo,* his legs shaking with the effort, his mind trying to separate the mists from reality. What should he do next? The sound of a motor cut through his thoughts, and he turned to see a jeep make a fast sweep out from behind the coffee shop and onto the road, heading toward Pattani. Silhouetted in the headlights, just for a second, was the figure of a woman — a woman who looked very much like Maggie Hathway. This thought filtered through the thick blanket of pain that surrounded Martin's thoughts, but the need to find help overwhelmed him like a tidal wave.

"Wait," Martin called out, trying to run after the jeep. "Wait for me!" He was positive that Jonas and Elizabeth were in that jeep, and he had no intention of being left behind. He wanted to run, but his legs refused to obey his command. He took three wobbly steps, hesitated, then fell face down on the ground, his senses protesting angrily at his weakness.

Just as darkness flooded his mind, he thought he heard Maggie calling his name; every effort to claw his way through the numbness invading his body failed. He was being sucked down into a deep, black pit from which no one ever returned.

The men who had witnessed his arrival silently surrounded the still figure on the ground, watching with far more curiosity than concern as he lay in an unconscious heap. Nor did they make any comments or offer to help the white woman who pushed her way through the crowd and threw herself down beside the foreigner, not even when she demanded medical assistance.

CHAPTER 15

Watchman, how far gone is the night?

The Prophet Isaiah

S u-Ling didn't waste any time letting them know what she
wanted.

"Go back to the house for the statue," she ordered.

"It's not there," Jonas growled.

"Yes, it is. Tell him, Elizabeth Thurston."

Su-Ling's words rang with exaltation as she gloated over
her information, but Elizabeth was more concerned with
Jonas's response. "I—I went after it."

"What!?" Jonas exploded. The jeep swerved to the left and
then back to the right. "Liz, what did you do?"

"Calm down," Elizabeth protested in nervous irritation. "I
thought—I knew—where Maggie had hidden it, and when Su-
Ling went into town, I, well, I found it. I just wanted to use it
as leverage for your release. It's the only way I could force
Chen to show us where you were."

No one spoke for a moment, then Jonas asked, "Did Maggie tell you where it was?"

"Well, not exactly. I sort of guessed."

"You sort of guessed," Jonas repeated, pushing the dark
hair from his forehead and trying to concentrate on the road

ahead. "I don't know whether I should be angry or just plain thankful! You could have been hurt."

"Wouldn't have missed it for anything," Elizabeth replied, keeping her voice light with effort. "It will be a great story for my grandchildren someday," she added, wondering if she would live long enough to have children.

Jonas reached over and squeezed her hand. He wanted so much to take her in his arms and tell her how proud he was of her, to help her see the courage she had displayed, to help her acknowledge the great love she had for others. But it would have to wait.

"Hurry," Su-Ling urged, glancing over her shoulder. "They will get all information from Chen and will come soon."

Silence reigned for the remainder of the trip back into Pattani, everyone contemplating in their own way the sobering thought of more confrontation and probable bloodshed. Finally, Jonas pulled up into the drive beside Maggie's house and cut the motor.

"Now what?" he asked, slipping the keys into his pocket. *If only I keep my wits about me,* he thought, *I should be able to find some way of getting that gun from Su-Ling.*

"Now, we go into the house," Su-Ling replied, jamming the gun into Elizabeth's back. "Do not do anything stupid, Jonas Adams. Elizabeth, light a lamp. Now, where did you hide the statue?"

"In the water pot in the washroom," Elizabeth replied with a shrug. At the time she had thought the huge container was an excellent hiding place; now it seemed a bit ridiculous.

"Get it," Su-Ling said tersely, her eyes glinting in the lamp-light as she moved around to the opposite side of the table. "If you do not obey me, one of you dies. Do not disobey me if you wish to live."

"You can't stay in control very long," Jonas challenged, his voice composed and forceful. Elizabeth turned her eyes full on him, drawn to his calmness. "Eventually you'll make a mistake. It's two against one."

"Do not think I am not wise," Su-Ling replied. "The numbers change; soon there will be just one of you."

It was a chilling warning. Elizabeth's eyes jumped from Su-Ling's taut expression to Jonas's face and found there the assurance she needed to search for the statue.

The clay pot stood waist high and was more than an arm's length across, and it was at least two-thirds full. Elizabeth eyed it dubiously for a moment before she began dipping out the water.

"Quickly," Su-Ling hissed, glancing out of the kitchen window. "They come soon!"

"I can't reach the bottom with all this water in it; I'm not tall enough."

"Stop pretending," Su-Ling warned, grabbing Elizabeth by the arm and throwing her down into a chair. Jonas lunged forward to intercept, but Su-Ling raised the gun and ordered, "Jonas Adams, *you* will get the statue."

They stared at each other for a long moment, Jonas trying to put a lid on his anger, Su-Ling coldly waiting. "Remember, I will shoot her if you do not obey." The tension mounted in response to Su-Ling's emotions; she was increasingly edgy and skittish, and her eyes darted around the room as though she expected trouble.

"All right, all right," Jonas replied, raising his hands in a conciliatory gesture as he moved slowly toward the washroom. "I'm going." He had no plans to sacrifice Elizabeth's life for a hunk of silver.

Thrusting his arm down into the water, he moved his hand slowly around the bottom and wondered for the first time what they would do if the statue wasn't there.

"Hurry!" Su-Ling spit out nervously in a way that was so unlike the Asian nature that Elizabeth was truly frightened. The woman was unpredictable and dangerous.

The gun barrel pushed deep into Elizabeth's back, and she sat erect, trying to move forward, away from that cold reminder of death that seemed to be continually prodding her flesh.

"Hurry!" Su-Ling demanded once more.

"Just stay calm," Jonas muttered, keeping an eye on the woman as he continued his search. Finally, his fingers touched a plastic bundle. Relieved, he brought it up out of the water and held it out toward Su-Ling like a dripping wet offering, waiting for her response.

"Put it on the table," she fumed. "Now open. I want to be sure you are not tricking me."

Jonas moved to the side of the table where she would have a clear view and opened the plastic bag, removed the sarong-wrapped bundle, and laid it on the table. When he gently pulled the sarong away from the statue, everyone gasped.

Without doubt, it was a beautiful piece of antiquity. Hundreds of years old and fashioned by hand, the silver-covered likeness of a former Thai king glittered in the lamplight. The detailed work on a statue no longer than a hand's length was amazing. Fashioned as a fierce warrior, the figure wore a short sword at his side, a dagger at his belt, and the emblem of royalty across his chest. It was without question a valuable item.

Jonas turned the statue over, just far enough for Elizabeth to see the back; a piece was missing.

"Wrap it up again," Su-Ling ordered, quite unaware of this non-verbal exchange of information. She deposited the statue in the straw tote bag she had left in the kitchen, slung it over her shoulder, and commanded, "We will go now."

"Just a minute," Jonas flared, indicating his torn shirt. "My back has been beaten raw. I don't plan on going anywhere without a change of clothes and a jacket."

"Very well," Su-Ling agreed reluctantly, "but remember that my gun is on your friend; do not try to find a weapon."

Jonas looked at her with a wry smile. "You needn't worry. I believe that's my gun you're using."

When he returned to the kitchen a few minutes later, he handed a sweater to Elizabeth, who sat shivering nervously in rain-soaked clothes. Su-Ling ordered him to fill the jeep tank with gasoline from cans Maggie kept locked up at the back of the house, then she forced them back into the jeep.

"Drive to the airport," she ordered. "We will use your plane to return to Bangkok."

Elizabeth swung around to protest. "No," she objected, staring in anger at Su-Ling. "We can't leave Martin and Maggie. We don't know what's happened to them and —"

Jonas interrupted. "I don't know how to fly," he objected, hoping to divert the woman. It was true; he wasn't a pilot. He had always hired someone, telling himself that as soon as he had time he would learn. And his recent escapade in Bangkok had certainly impressed on him that he shouldn't wait any longer. But he would not attempt to fly that plane with Elizabeth aboard.

"Listen," he urged, "less than a month ago I had to make an emergency landing after the pilot was shot, but I did it with instructions from the radio tower. I will not try that again!" *That should put a kink in her plans,* he thought.

But she simply laughed at him. "I have license to fly, Jonas Adams. It will be no problem. You will be my prisoner if we find trouble."

Jonas frowned but threw the jeep into reverse, backed out into the street, and headed for the airport. The empty streets mocked Elizabeth's hope that they might find help from someone in town; even the police station looked vacant. It was nearing daybreak, and the morning market would soon fill with early shoppers. But that would not help them now. If only they could have come through town a half hour later!

No matter how diligently she worked to think of some scheme, fortuitous or otherwise, her mind seemed void of coherent thought. No intelligent idea dropped into her mind, no plan from God's direction. Nothing. All she could do was berate her stupidity at laying the gun down and then forgetting all about it. No agent, no spy, not even a neophyte adventurer — *nobody* in their right mind would have done such a foolish thing. But she had.

When they neared the airfield, Su-Ling leaned forward with excitement — she was so near success — and directed Jonas to pull the jeep into the shadows of the frangipani bushes that bordered one side of the airfield.

The airport was deserted, the unpretentious terminal building still locked up for the night, one small light burning over the front entrance. The cement runway stood empty, and no trucks were parked anywhere in the area. The only plane, the jet belonging to Jonas Adams, stood poised on the field like a sleek, silver rocket awaiting the dawn. It was a peaceful scene: no beatings, no warring factions, no demands at gunpoint, nothing but silence.

"Get out of the jeep, Jonas Adams," Su-Ling ordered softly. "Go open your plane."

Jonas directed a gentle glance toward Elizabeth before stepping out of the jeep. Slowly he advanced across the airfield, wondering just how far he could push Su-Ling's increasing nervousness before it backfired on them, and thinking that this was truly a case of *déjà vu*; he had been through this just a few weeks ago at the Bangkok airport. Now he was once more about to become a hostage in an airplane.

Not expecting to see any officials around, he still prayed that something or someone might distract Su-Ling. But he wasn't prepared for the distraction that came.

A sense of dread washed over Elizabeth as she watched him walk toward the plane — an unexplainable horror that made her heart hammer, a terror she couldn't control. "Jonas, stop!" she called out.

He whirled around, expecting to see her in trouble.

"Quiet!" Su-Ling hissed, her anger boiling over. "Do you want me to kill you now?"

Suddenly, over Su-Ling's orders and Elizabeth's protests came the roaring sound of an explosion. They turned as one person to stare in shock across the airfield. In one second the ultra-modern jet and the airport building burst into flames like a tremendous jigsaw puzzle being ripped apart and tossed into the sky by some angry giant. Pieces of cement building and metal airplane flew in all directions. Explosion followed explosion as flying debris hit the stockpile of gasoline drums.

The first blast tossed Jonas up into the air and back into a pile of empty gasoline drums. He fell like a wet towel torn from a clothes line. Elizabeth screamed and tried to get out of the jeep. "Let me go!" she kept pleading, ignoring the gun at her head and the threats from Su-Ling.

Sirens began to wail, and the frightened occupants of nearby houses suddenly filled the streets. Shouts and screams swelled the air. Total confusion dominated the scene, engulfing Su-Ling for a few moments. Her one way of immediate escape had just blown up in her face; she had no contingency plan, but she knew there had to be some other way out of town.

"Is the road to Yala closed with the rainy season?"

"I don't know," Elizabeth moaned, her eyes still on the still form lying on the ground. "And I don't care!"

"Where is the road?"

"It's the one that goes past Maggie's house, I think," Elizabeth supplied reluctantly, her voice full of tears, and her attention entirely upon Jonas.

"We will go," Su-Ling said. "Drive the jeep."

Elizabeth stared at her as though she were faced with a monster. "Are you crazy?!"

"I am leaving this town!"

"Well, I won't drive! Do it yourself!" Elizabeth shouted. "If you've killed Jonas, I'll . . ." For a moment, Elizabeth's anger swept away common sense. "I don't care what you do, or how many silver statues you steal, or how many Malays are after you, I won't drive!"

But the cold stare of hatred that met her eyes from the back seat forced Elizabeth to acknowledge that she would help no one if she were dead. She slumped forward for a moment, then reluctantly moved over to the driver's side and turned the key in the ignition.

This night was worse than the most terrifying of nightmares. First she had left Martin bleeding to death in some unknown hut in the jungle; now she was leaving Jonas lying unconscious on the ground while explosions and fire raged around him. She could not expect to survive the night nor Su-Ling's determination. And she really didn't care. Jonas, the one man on earth who had met the deep longing in her heart, who knew how to fill the emptiness, whose eyes had promised to love her forever, was dead.

On the return trip through town the streets were filled with people, but none of them paid any attention to the jeep as they all ran pell-mell toward the airport to see the destruction firsthand.

Not long after they passed Maggie's house and were out in the open countryside, Elizabeth glanced into the rear view mirror. "There's a jeep following us," she said, her voice devoid of feelings.

Su-Ling stared over her shoulder at the headlights behind them and finally muttered, more to herself than to her driver, "Two jeeps!" She turned her attention back to Elizabeth.

"For now, you are safer with me than with them. You must know that! I will not kill you unless you give me trouble. They—" she jerked her chin toward her left shoulder, " would enjoy cutting you into small pieces, after they have had their pleasure! Now, go!"

The warning penetrated Elizabeth's numbness, and knowing there must be a justification for the sacrifice of those she loved, she jammed her foot down on the accelerator and whipped the jeep around the next curve. The lights in the rear view mirror disappeared.

It was a wild, exhausting drive. Elizabeth kept her foot down hard on the gas pedal, saw the speedometer needle climb dangerously, and enjoyed the frightened expression on Su-Ling's face. For a moment, she entertained the thought of swerving hard enough to the left to throw her captor out of the jeep. But Su-Ling had evidently anticipated that; she was braced against such a possibility, feet hard up against the jeep floor, one hand clinging to the seat, the other holding the gun.

Elizabeth's foot hardly touched the brakes, even for the curve which they took in a slide across the wet black top while she prayed there would be no oncoming traffic. It was time for the early buses that carried people to country markets for the day, and she had no wish to end up as a victim of a traffic disaster.

They sped past a rubber plantation; the tall, slender trees were a blur of pale brown bark tattooed with white slashes which marked the place where the latex seeped down into small buckets. Down the long, straight stretches of road they were again nagged by the trailing jeeps. At one point she thought she heard gun shots, and Su-Ling's angry confirmation in scrambled English verified her fears.

"Faster! Guns are shooting!"

Elizabeth obeyed, and after awhile her motions became mechanical, changing gears to pick up speed or to take a sharp curve, guiding the jeep around groups of rubber tappers on their way to work, pulling past the slow-moving *samlos* whenever they neared a village. Her thoughts were on Jonas, and she feared that he was dead. His image, his smile was stamped irrevocably in her mind, and she fought down the emptiness that threatened to engulf her as she envisioned never seeing him alive again. Then another concern brought her mind back sharply to her present reality.

Sprinting into a small village of four or five houses and a couple of shops at a curve in the road, Elizabeth let up slightly on the gas pedal, slapped her hand down on the horn, and kept it there — a long, grating blast of warning that the early risers meandering along the roadside toward the coffee shops should stay clear.

All the way she had prayed that she wouldn't encounter a country bus whose drivers were all demons behind the wheel, fighting insanely to be the first to pick up passengers in the next village. But she rounded the next corner and without warning came sliding up behind a vehicle overflowing with people and produce. Once more her hand went down on the horn, and she jerked the jeep into the outside lane to pull around the bus. But it was only a challenge to the driver.

She had thrown down the glove, she had dared to question his abilities, and as far as he was concerned, it was a duel to the end. He threw the bus into low gear to pick up speed; the men hanging on the back of the overcrowded bus egged him on with shouts and laughter.

After several long, terrifying minutes, Elizabeth saw a narrow bridge in the road ahead. Jeep and bus hurtled toward it like rockets blasting into space, each driver determined to reach it first. She threw the jeep into low gear and rammed the gas pedal to the floor again.

For a long moment, jeep and bus flew down the road together, sending puddles of water spewing up into the air, neither one giving an inch. Elizabeth, disregarding the shrieks coming from the bus and ignoring Su-Ling, gripped the wheel tightly and held her mind on the goal. If she could get ahead, traffic behind them would be stuck behind the bus, and even five minutes would give her a good edge.

Finally, when she was about ready to give up, when the bridge seemed to be rushing toward them with uncontrollable speed, she felt the jeep pull ahead. With a complimentary blast of the horn, the other driver capitulated with a grin. She whipped the jeep over in front of the bus at the last moment, tore over the bridge, and soon left her competition behind.

For twenty minutes or so the road behind them was empty. Elizabeth forced her body to relax, knowing she was preparing for the next encounter. And then, just as they tore into the edges of the city of Yala, their pursuers reappeared from nowhere. There was the sound of gunfire, and a second later a bullet whipped past Elizabeth's ear and slapped into the windshield. She gasped, almost losing control of the jeep, and then turned sharply at the next corner onto the road that passed the railroad station. The overnight train from Bangkok, on its way to the southern border of Thailand, was about to pull out of the station.

"Turn there," Su-Ling ordered sharply.

Elizabeth jerked the steering wheel, barely missing the corner of a building, and pulled into a narrow alley.

"Stop!" Su-Ling was standing on the ground beside the jeep before Elizabeth had brought it to a full stop. "Get out!"

Su-Ling pulled Elizabeth in front of her as a shield and edged out of the alley. By some unknown miracle, the other jeeps had missed them and were roaring down the road, heading into the downtown section of the city. But Su-Ling didn't intend to wait for them to discover their mistake. She ran toward the last car of the train, dodging other passengers and pulling Elizabeth with her. The tote bag, heavy with the silver statue, cut into her shoulder, making it difficult to push Elizabeth up the steps and onto the train. They were barely on the platform before the train began to move.

If their pursuers decided to board the train at some point along the line, it would likely be on the last car in order to make a thorough search. Su-Ling forced Elizabeth through the crowded aisles until they were nearer the middle section of the train. Finally, she indicated that they could stop.

Elizabeth sank down in an empty seat, closed her eyes, and began to shake uncontrollably. None of her college friends would ever believe the long, sleepless night she had just been through, and, regrettably, she saw no bright promises for the day ahead. Indifferent to the disturbance their presence caused, she left the problems of the conductor and the questions fired at them by curious passengers to Su-Ling; she clamped her jaw tightly and concentrated on getting her shivering body under control.

The train settled into a fast pace toward the border town of Sungei Golok. Somewhere along the way she must have dropped off to sleep, for she was suddenly aware of Su-Ling prodding her awake with the warning that Haji Met's son and a companion were standing at the far end of the car.

"They have seen us," Su-Ling murmured, her hand tightening on the gun in her tote bag. "Sit still, Elizabeth Thurston, and do nothing!"

Elizabeth threw her a wry glance. "Just what do you think I want to do?" she asked. "I'm not too happy being your prisoner, but I certainly don't wish to be theirs." She saw Haji Met's son sit down where he could keep them in full view; the other man left the car, probably to report to someone else on the train.

"Tell me," she continued, "what do you plan to do when we get to Sungei Golok? If I remember correctly, that's the end of the line. You'll have to change to another train—whenever it decides to arrive — in order to get over the border and into Malaya. And I assume that's what you've had in mind all along."

Su-Ling nodded curtly, her eyes on the far end of the car. "It is."

"Someone waiting for you there?"

"Too many questions are not safe," the Chinese woman replied softly.

"But let me ask another one. How do you plan to get off this train, keep me as a hostage, and then get over the border before feeling Haji Met's gun in your back? They'll be all over us before we step off the train."

"Look around you, Elizabeth Thurston," Su-Ling replied dryly. "Most train passengers smuggle goods across the border. And the police cannot arrest them unless they have the goods in their hands." She nodded toward a Malay carrying half a dozen Thai umbrellas and a Chinese holding a package wrapped in newspaper which could contain items made from Thai silver.

"Better prices in Malaya, and more if they do not go through customs."

"Why don't the police catch them?"

"The smugglers wait until the customs man goes through the car, then they move their goods around; they never stay in the same place. When the train stops in Sungei Golok, everyone runs for trees or the river. Haji Met will not fire on his own people, and we will be in the middle of them."

The vision of all this mayhem, with policemen chasing smugglers and Malay insurrectionists chasing Su-Ling, gave Elizabeth a lot to think about. It would be the perfect time for her to get away from Su-Ling and disappear into the crowd. This hope calmed her heart when they slowly pulled into the Sungei Golok station, and Su-Ling grabbed the back of her blouse and pushed her down the steps and off the train.

But hope sometimes dies quickly. A man's hand, brandishing a knife, came snaking into view toward Su-Ling's gun. "Stop now!" he ordered in broken English, reaching out to grab Elizabeth's shoulder. In one blurred motion Su-Ling turned, grabbed the man next to her by the arm, and hurled him, suitcase and all, into the assailant's body. Then she ran, pulling Elizabeth with her. Shouts and protests surged up from some of the passengers; others complacently ignored the problem and continued silently toward the railroad bridge — the border marker that spanned the river between the two countries.

They were within twenty yards of the bridge when bullets lacerated the ground around their feet. Su-Ling stopped, jerked Elizabeth around as a shield, and then began backing toward the river.

"I will kill her," she shouted. "Stay away, or I will kill her."

CHAPTER 16

*And its end will come with a
flood.*

The Prophet Daniel

Fumes . . . charred metal. . . exploding gasoline. Choking
smells invaded Jonas's consciousness like stinging acid.
He needed air, but his lungs fought each searing breath. Despite
intense physical pain a more intense concern overwhelmed him.
Where was Elizabeth? What had happened to her? Had the jeep
been hit by flying metal? Through the haze and stench and heat
he tried to focus his mind on the need to move. If only he could
get up, he could go to Elizabeth's rescue! But his mind refused
to function, his body felt like a ton of rock.

"Elizabeth," he groaned, staggering to his feet. But the
acute pain in his head sent him sprawling forward, knocking
drums everywhere.

The unfathomable blackness swirled into a deep green, then
gray, then . . . He opened his eyes. He couldn't have been unconscious for more than a few minutes, for the fire and heat
still raged. This time he could hear sirens and shouted commands and the thud of feet as people converged on the airfield.

As he tried unsuccessfully to move once again, he realized
that he lay under a toppled pyramid of empty gasoline drums.

Too heavy to budge, the drums still held enough gasoline to explode if the fire came any nearer.

He tried to concentrate on the danger, but his mind drifted into a timeless space. Important events and people from his life flashed with lightning speed before his mind in sharp, painful detail. He saw his marriage to Lian and remembered his first knowledge of the horrifying disease that had taken her life. Her face floated briefly before him — dark, Oriental eyes, a gentle smile that held an intriguing mystique he had so loved. Then the image faded — just as her life had faded even though he had begged her to stay — and another face took its place.

It was the face of the young American woman who had come into his life with a prickliness hiding a gentle, compassionate spirit — a spirit that made his own complete in a way his dear Lian would never have been able to do. Oh, Elizabeth, how I love you, how I need you.

In splintered thoughts, his love for Elizabeth was mixed with his pleadings to God. *Elizabeth, I love you . . . be near me, Lord, I'm not afraid . . . Elizabeth, can't you hear me . . . Lord, be my refuge and shield . . . Kindred spirits, Liz, that's what we are, can't you see it . . . Beautiful questioning eyes . . . Lord, my stronghold in trouble . . . Let me live, for her . . . Liz.*

Once more the blackness flooded his mind, its strength seeping into his body and seeming to stop the heartbeat and flow of blood. Jonas wondered if this was the passage of death to eternity beyond. If so, he would have to give in; he could not resist its power.

He heard an urgent voice. "Jonas Adams. Jonas Adams!"

Jonas wondered if he were hallucinating in his final moments of life. He reached out to touch death, but his hand sank into darkness; his entire body fell into ebony space. He could see and feel nothing but the pain in his head.

"Jonas Adams!"

But Jonas Adams could not respond.

ია. ია. ია.

Elizabeth Thurston entertained no illusions about her
chances of survival. As Haji Met's men closed in, Su-Ling desperately pulled her toward a bridge that symbolized certain disaster. Inexorably, she was being sucked into the climax of this
endless night of peril, and she wondered how she could possibly react appropriately with a mind numb from exhaustion.

Su-Ling stepped up on the railroad bridge, grabbed Elizabeth by the silver belt, and jerked her around as a shield. In her
haste she misjudged the distance between the widely-spaced
railroad ties. Stepping backward, her leg slipped through a
crack, and she fell, taking Elizabeth with her.

Elizabeth groaned at the impact and threw a hand out over
the wide, empty space between the railroad ties and the supports that spanned the bridge. Her fingers brushed the metal
piece, but Su-Ling's weight was dragging her downward. In a
moment, they would both lose their footing and tumble into the
swift current of the flood waters below.

She threw her body to the left, one hand clawing the air,
the other hanging onto the belt at her waist. Finally, despite all
the extra weight, she managed to grasp the support and help Su-
Ling back up on the bridge. Then she slumped against the railing, too weak to do anything but silently thank God for His
help.

"Wh-why did you h-help me?" Su-Ling gasped, gulping in
deep breaths of air.

"You could have drowned," Elizabeth replied simply and
without hesitation. Her eyes were closed, and she did not see
the look of surprised longing that flashed over Su-Ling's face.
She was aware only of the roar of the rushing river and the
shifting of the bridge as it gave in to the force of the torrent
below. She caught sight of smugglers prudently swerving away
from the bridge and making toward the safety of the jungle.

Haji Met and his men remained in the open field; and they advanced slowly, almost swaggering with confidence. At that moment Elizabeth silently agreed with them; it looked as though they were about to recapture the silver statue, and she didn't think they would hesitate to kill two women to get what they wanted.

Hasim circled around to the left while Haji Met signaled others to move to the right, their guns ready.

"Put down the silver statue," Haji Met called out, "or we will shoot you."

Elizabeth knew he meant it. "Put it down, Su-Ling. You'll never get off this bridge alive if you don't! It isn't worth it. Put it down."

"Never!" Su-Ling hissed in her ear. She took another step backward, pulling Elizabeth with her.

Haji Met raised a hand. In a moment he would call out the order to shoot. Elizabeth held her breath and waited.

Suddenly, an army truck pulled up beside the railroad station, and men wearing the uniform of the Thai border police poured out of the back and fanned out across the field, their guns aimed at the Moslem insurgents. But Haji Met's men were too close to their goal to stop now. They ignored the commands to halt, advancing slowly across the field.

A jeep sped through the mass of *samlos* waiting to transport train passengers back into town, scattering Haji Met's men like frightened monkeys before a charging elephant. It slid to a halt in the mud beside the bridge, and two men hopped out. The driver leaped onto the railroad tracks and aimed his gun at a startled Su-Ling.

"Chen!" she cried, and then laughed. "You came at the right time. Keep them away while I cross the river."

"I cannot do that," he responded.

Quietly, Chen's passenger stepped around the end of the bridge into view.

"Jonas!" Elizabeth exclaimed and started forward. A wave of unbelievable relief brought stinging tears to her eyes. He was still alive — battered and obviously in pain, clothes torn, face lacerated, but standing there — alive. "Oh, Jonas, are you all right?"

Silently, he raised a hand of warning and sent her a warm but weary smile. His hand brushed the dark hair from his forehead — a familiar gesture he used when he was troubled. In a choking voice she whispered his name.

Intent on being reassured that he hadn't been harmed in the fire, Elizabeth did not question his presence with Chen, a man who had claimed to be a Communist agent and who had only a few hours before threatened to take her life. She wanted to ignore the terrible events of the moment and run to the security of Jonas's arms. She wanted to hear how much he loved her.

Her thoughts were interrupted abruptly as Su-Ling tightened her grip on the belt and began to bargain with Chen.

"Stop Haji Met. Let me cross the bridge. Half of the money will be yours."

Chen shook his head. "No, I cannot do that."

"Then I will throw the statue into the river," she cried triumphantly, holding her tote bag out over the water. "No one will get it! I will escape into Malaysia, and you will be killed by our superiors! You will die!"

Elizabeth shivered against the cruel laughter spilling out between Su-Ling's words as she shouted, "Come, get it!"

"I don't want it."

"Why not?" Su-Ling demanded, suddenly wary.

"The statue is fake."

The authority in Chen's quiet response brought the world to a standstill. Haji Met grunted and Hasim swore loudly. Su-Ling's anger cut through the silence that signaled the Haji's capitulation to this turn of events.

"I do not believe it!" she spat out.

Chen shrugged his shoulders Asian-style. "I am an agent for Colonel Chandrung. We knew the UMF" — he nodded toward Haji Met "and the Communists" — then he turned his eyes on Su-Ling — "would do anything for political gain. We have been infiltrating your ranks for a long time."

"Then, you sent the — " Elizabeth stopped abruptly, thinking of the box she had received in Bangkok.

"Sent what?" Su-Ling demanded.

Elizabeth had almost mentioned the silver piece, and she tore through her thoughts for a diversion. "You sent my telegram to the hospital so that Maggie would know of my arrival."

Chen nodded. "Yes."

Su-Ling, irritated with information that wasn't pertinent to her plans, interrupted them. "Chen, you lie to save your own life. You failed. Now you try to get the statue for yourself."

"No," the government agent replied. "The best way to catch a tiger is to lure it out into the open. Our agency put out a report that a certain statue would be taken from Thonburi to the royal museum."

Su-Ling laughed. "I am not stupid. I have information sources as well, and they say the statue is authentic. Now I am to believe your words?!"

"Yes," Jonas cut in. He stepped forward for a clearer view of the two women. "The statue isn't any good. Look at it," he urged, intent on convincing Su-Ling of the truth. "There's a piece missing on the back, and it's the only part that's important. It's engraved with an inscription in an ancient language. *That's* what's valuable!"

Elizabeth drew in a sharp breath, and quickly touched her belt; the silver piece was still there.

Su-Ling noticed this unconscious reflex, and her eyes narrowed reflectively. "If this is true," she said, eyeing the silver belt, "where is the missing piece?" Her eyes darted to Chen's impassive face, then to Jonas's concerned expression, and finally caught the defiance in Elizabeth's eyes. And then she knew.

She reached for the belt, but Elizabeth fought her off, pulling away and trying to stay out of her grasp. The women teetered precariously on the edge of the tracks. It was the moment Jonas had been waiting for, and he leaped forward. The swaying, buckling bridge hampered his progress, and when Su-Ling saw him, she shouted, "Come any closer and I will kill her!"

"No!" Jonas stopped instantly and spread his hands open so that she could see that he did not have a weapon. "I'll make a bargain with you. Release her, and we'll let you go free."

"You will *let* me go! I have the hostage, and you will let me go!" Su-Ling laughed at his audacity.

"Have you forgotten about the soldiers behind us?" he asked. "Every one of them has a gun. You won't make it to the end of the bridge."

Su-Ling glanced contemptuously over the line of border patrol. "Do you think they can shoot me and miss Elizabeth Thurston — or you?" With a shrug she dismissed that threat. She knew Chen would not issue an order that would endanger the lives of two Americans. She turned to Elizabeth. "Give me the belt," she demanded.

Jonas nodded. "Let her have it, Liz."

Reluctantly, Elizabeth released the belt clasp, folded it up link by link, and held it out in the palm of her hand.

Just as Su-Ling reached for the belt, the bridge supports wrenched violently, the rails twisting and turning like a living snake. Su-Ling grabbed for the railing, her attention diverted from Elizabeth and the soldiers.

Elizabeth, thrown forward to her knees, hung on to the railroad tracks to keep from slipping into the water. With a sudden roar the water surged around a bend and hit the structure with terrifying force. The bridge itself crackled sharply, moaning as metal scraped against metal. The ties beneath Su-Ling's feet split in two, and the rails bent sharply downward. Then they snapped.

The belt flew into the air. Ignoring her own safety, Su-Ling lunged forward to catch it and lost her balance as the belt hit the surging water and disappeared. Su-Ling hung from the railings, the heavy statue in her tote bag slowly pulling her downward.

Jonas saw the tracks beginning to buckle up in front of him, blocking his way as the bridge yielded to the demands of the flooding river. He jumped forward, hoping the structure would hold his weight long enough for him to grab Elizabeth.

"Su-Ling, let me help you," Elizabeth cried, trying to reach down between the broken rails.

"No! I will die in the water. I will not be shot down like a common criminal!" Su-Ling spat out scornfully.

"Please, I want to help you," Elizabeth begged, almost losing her balance as she strained forward. "God loves you. He can help. See with your heart, Su-Ling. Open your heart to His love. Please! Please, don't let go!"

Elizabeth was sobbing now, afraid she was going to fail to reach Su-Ling's mind. It was the woman's bitterness that pulled her toward death, not the river nor a bullet from Chen's gun.

"God loves you," she repeated.

"You lie!" Su-Ling screamed. "You Christians always lie! Your God is not alive; He cannot help anyone. You lie!"

"No!" Elizabeth responded quickly, shouting above the noise of the crumbling bridge and the rushing current below. "No, Su-Ling, He died for you! He wants you to believe that. He wants you to be His child. He can give you eternal life. Believe it, oh, please, believe it!"

Elizabeth stared into the hatred of Su-Ling's disbelief, silently pouring her love out toward the woman, willing her to accept the truth. For a brief moment, a hungry look flooded Su-Ling's face, like a little girl longing for some great gift. Her eyes bright with hope, she stared back at Elizabeth. Then it vanished, replaced by the animosity that had driven her to this point in her life.

"I hate your God," she hissed.

Elizabeth plunged forward over the broken railroad tracks in a final attempt to rescue Su-Ling, but she was too late. Su-Ling screamed angrily at the "Christian God" and let go of the railings, plunging straight down and disappearing beneath the raging waters.

Elizabeth's last effort to catch Su-Ling had pulled her out too far. Her body slid down the railings, and there was nothing she could grab to stop her fall.

"Jonas!" she cried. "Jonas, help me!"

Someone grabbed her feet and then caught her hand, and she was hoisted back up onto the bridge. In the next moment she was huddled in Jonas's arms, her face buried in his chest, her arms clinging to him as she tried to stop the sobbing that shook her body.

"It's all right, Liz," he murmured, holding her tightly in his arms, pouring out his love and reassurance, giving her time to regain control of her emotions before they fought their way back across the bridge to safety.

"I couldn't help her, Jonas," she sobbed. "I lost her. She just wouldn't believe me."

"I know." Jonas didn't try to deny the painful truth nor minimize the depth of her caring. His comfort and acceptance of her pain soothed her spirit, and she stopped crying. "Come on, my love, let's get back to safety," he urged, turning to face the precarious walk through twisted metal and dangling, broken railroad ties.

"We're going to make it, honey. We're going to make it all the way."

&ā &ā &ā

That same afternoon a special police team escorted Jonas and Elizabeth back to the Pattani hospital, a sprawling, one-story complex of Thai architecture with pointed rooftops and delicate lattice work, built high off the ground for comfort. The Asian nurse at the front desk directed them to a private room at the end of the right wing. There they found Maggie seated beside the bed, holding Martin's hand as he slept.

The moment she saw them, she broke into a relieved smile and hurried to the door. "Am I glad to see you two!" she whispered, her voice breaking. She held Elizabeth for a long moment, both of them crying a little, and then gave Jonas a hug. "Thank God you're safe. I was so afraid for you."

"How is he, Maggie?" Elizabeth asked as she looked toward the bed where Martin rested.

"The doctor says he's going to be fine." Maggie whispered, her voice still shaking with emotion. "He had a blood transfusion. But I'll tell you something: I wasn't so sure he was going to live when I found him."

As they walked slowly toward the bed, Maggie told her story. "Haji Met wasn't interested in any more hostages. He wanted Su-Ling. He had one of the villagers bring us into Pattani. And I told the man that if he didn't take us straight to the hospital, I would report him to the governor!"

Martin turned his head, and with his eyes still closed, murmured, "She would have, too. Jonas, going to have my hands full. What a whirlwind she is." He reached for Maggie's hand and grinned. "But I like challenges."

Maggie's eyes sparkled as she leaned over the bed. "I don't think you'd win any battles today."

"Oh, no?" Martin opened his eyes, and the look between them spoke of satisfaction and understanding. When Maggie leaned over to kiss him gently on the lips, he smiled. "Score one for me," he said before he sighed and gave into the weakness he would battle for several days.

After relating briefly what had taken place on the wild chase to Sungei Golok and the climax at the border, Jonas sorted out all the people for Martin. "Su-Ling was working for a Chinese group, and Chen, a government agent, was connected with the local Chinese church. And, of course, the others were involved with the UMF. Quite a mix-up!"

Later, Jonas and Elizabeth left Martin's room and went for a walk on the hospital grounds. They found a small, enclosed garden that was empty of hospital patients because of the supper hour. The rains had stopped, and the sun was sinking rapidly, as it does in the Orient. It painted the sky with an expertise beyond that of human artistry, changing the colors from brilliant pinks to reds and purples before darkness came.

In a comfortable silence, Jonas pulled Elizabeth down on a bench and took her in his arms. He held her for a long moment, rejoicing in God's protection for them, immensely relieved just to feel her presence. "Elizabeth Thurston," he murmured, "the more I know about you, the more I love you. God has brought us together, and you fill my life, you make it complete."

"Jonas . . ." she began hesitantly.

Jonas pulled away and looked down into her face. "I really believe I was near death, Liz, after being knocked to the ground by the explosions at the airport. My life flashed before me in seconds. I saw my wife Lian, just briefly, but it was your image that gave me courage to fight for my life. Your face, your gentle eyes. It was almost as if you were begging me not to give in."

"I — I don't know what I would have done," Elizabeth whispered. "I don't know what I would do without you." She had more to say, and she put a hand up to stop his kiss. "I don't think," she said slowly, her eyes full of wonder, "that there is another man on this earth who could touch my soul like you have. I still find it difficult to believe, much less understand. How does that happen, Jonas?"

"Oh, my love," Jonas replied as he pulled her closer, "I plan to take a lifetime explaining that to you. I want you to depend on my love. You don't need to be afraid that once you truly trust me, I'll go looking for someone else. I want our life together to be one that will encourage others and honor the Lord." He tipped her face up, searched it with deep satisfaction, and then kissed her again and again.

After several minutes he murmured, "Liz, you will marry me, won't you?"

Elizabeth looked up, and he could see a smile teasing her lips and deepening the love in her eyes.

"Only on one condition." Her eyes sparkled with a new-found freedom in his love.

"What's that?" he asked suspiciously.

"That you pay for my karate lessons."

"Your what?"

"Well, if you expect me to marry someone who's always being chased by the bad guys, you must agree that I've got to have some kind of protection!"

"I'll protect you well enough," he growled, and pulled her close once more.

ABOUT THE AUTHOR

J ean Springer lives and writes in Elkhart, Indiana. She has earned a Bachelor of Theology degree from Southeastern Bible College and has previously published three novels with Bethel Publishing. Jean also has coordinated conferences, taught seminars, and held private classes on writing.

Jean and her husband, Myron, have raised four daughters, and from 1957 until 1960, they were in South Thailand, working primarily among the Malay Moslems.

The typeface for the text of this book is *Times Roman*. In 1930, typographer Stanley Morison joined the staff of *The Times* (London) to supervise design of a typeface for the reformatting of this renowned English daily. Morison had overseen type-library reforms at Cambridge University Press in 1925, but this new task would prove a formidable challenge despite a decade of experience in paleography, calligraphy, and typography. *Times New Roman* was credited as coming from Morison's original pencil renderings in the first years of the 1930s, but the typeface went through numerous changes under the scrutiny of a critical committee of dissatisfied *Times* staffers and editors. The resulting typeface, *Times Roman*, has been called the most used, most successful typeface of this century. The design is of enduring value to English and American printers and publishers, who choose the typeface for its readability and economy when run on today's high-speed presses.

Substantive Editing:
Michael S. Hyatt

Copy Editing:
Peggy Moon

Cover Design:
Steve Diggs & Friends
Nashville, Tennessee

Page Composition:
Xerox Ventura Publisher
Printware 720 IQ Laser Printer

Printing and Binding:
Maple-Vail Book Manufacturing Group
York, Pennsylvania

Trade Printing:
Weber Graphics
Chicago, Illinois